Tiepolo's Greyhound

An Artworld Adventure

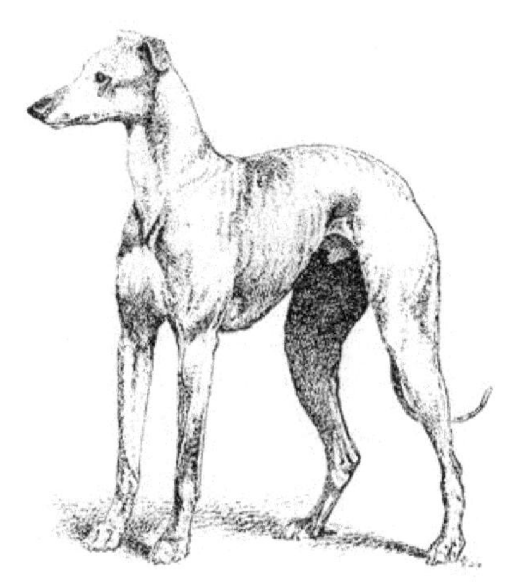

Contact: editor@bookbogglers.us
ISBN 979-8-9885865-31

Front cover: Viola Wake 2023
Back cover image: Giovanni Domenico Tiepolo 1791

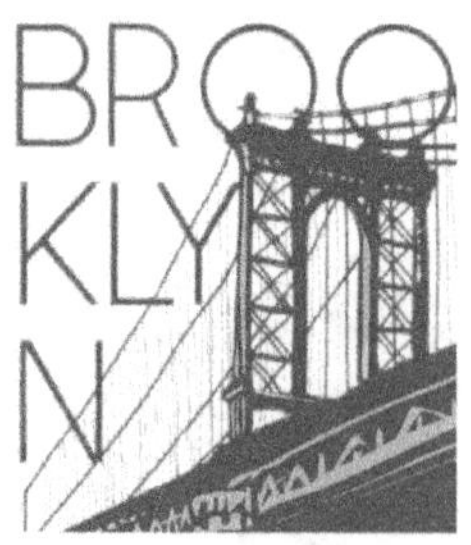

A Brooklyn Story
Imprint of Book Bogglers
www.bookbogglers.us

Dedication

To Anthony Benedetto, “the great singer of New York—whose own father, born in Calabria, had long ago packed a suitcase and prepared for this same journey. He like Alfonso must have had to find a way to say good-bye.”

–Piccolo Fortunato

Tiepolo's Greyhound

To the Kinship of All Species

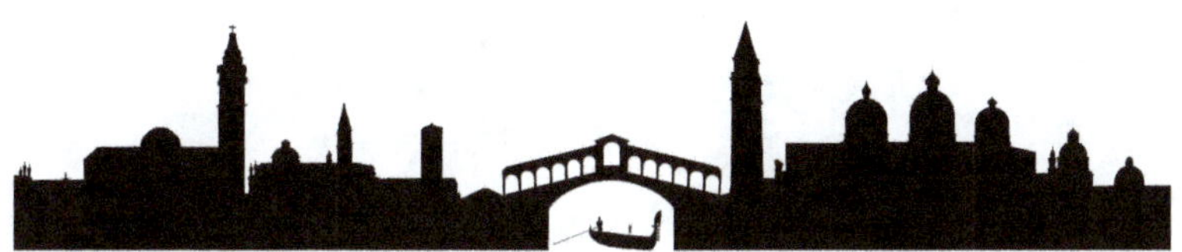

"Celebrating artistic pursuits… with a clear sense of whimsy as canine characters wear porkpie hats, lap up wine, sing Frank Sinatra tunes, and yearn for romance. Along the way, the author also effectively skewers the modern-day art world—particularly its use of interns. Ultimately, this book is most effective as a joyful appreciation of Venice and great art." *–Kirkus Reviews*

"The writing is smart, sly, and very effective, and I found myself laughing out loud at the sheer verve and nerve of the narrative and the voice. In a sea of standard mysteries and genre books, this one clearly stands out." *–Writer's Digest Competition Review*

"Skillfully the author weaves in artworld enticements and disappointments with such twists of humor and layers of insight readers get a chance to feel what it might be like to crave success in that mad race to be part of the NYC art scene." *–Arteidolia*

Illustrations by Veronica Arrigoni

Like Piccolo, Veronica Arrigoni is an artist of Italy as well as a spirited educator and toymaker.

da Castelfranco, Giorgione (1506). *The Tempest* [oil on canvas]. Gallerie dell'Accademia, Venice, Italy.

di Suvero, Mark (1983–1989). *For Gerald Manley Hopkins* [painted steel]. Collection of Hansol Foundation of Culture, Seoul, Seoul, Korea.

Fortunato, Piccolo (2003). *Sniff* [steel]. Private Collection, Brooklyn, New York.

Tiepolo, Giovanni Domenico (1791). *Mondo Nuovo* [fresco]. Ca'Rezzonico, Venice, Italy.

Tiepolo, Giovanni Domenico (1793). *Italian Greyhound* [fresco]. Ca'Rezzonico, Venice, Italy.

Tiepolo, Giovanni Domenico (1793). *Swing of Pulcinella* [fresco]. Ca'Rezzonico, Venice, Italy.

Tintoretto, Jacopo Robusti (1551). *Creation of the Animals* [oil on canvas]. Gallerie dell'Accademia, Venice, Italy.

Tintoretto, Jacopo Robusti (1548). *Miracle of the Slave* [oil on canvas]. Gallerie dell'Accademia, Venice, Italy.

unknown Roman artist. (1^{st}CE-2nd CE). *Townley Greyhounds* [marble]. British Museum, London, England.

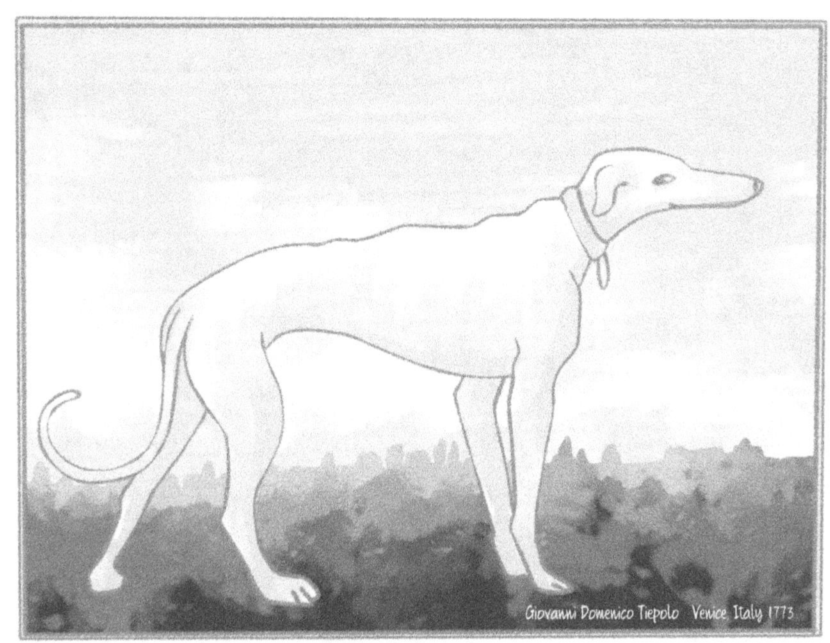

CONTENTS

1 From Venice

Call me Piccolo. Born in Venice at the turn of this century, I am the descendant of a proud family of Italian greyhounds who have lived for many generations in Cannaregio, a quiet neighborhood of morning markets and small cafes beside the Grand Canal.

My father Alfonso Fortunato is a sculptor who as a young dog worked in the boatyard of the Tramontin family whose gondolas are still handcrafted in the age-old tradition. Back in the fifth century, the ancestors of both our families fled the mainland when barbarian hordes ravaged the fields and burned down their villages. Settling on the marshes of the lagoon, they drove tree trunks into the mud to make foundations for their huts and ovens. Over time, working by their side, we Fortunatos helped to build the canals, courtyards, palazzos and cathedrals of Venice, providing our city with artisans skilled in mosaic, metal work and glassblowing.

If you are to understand my story, I must make something very clear. It was through the adaptations of time and the exquisite use of our paws that we Fortunatos developed dexterity far beyond any breed—as well as a tolerance and taste for the wine we drank from the goatskin sack with our fellow workers.

And so, in keeping with the family tradition, my father taught me from a young age to carve the wood, chisel the stone and with the small blue flame of my torch to cut and weld the steel.

My mother Isabella was renowned for her gracious nature and the sheen of her fawn and cream-colored coat. Often she has told me of our ancestor who long ago apprenticed in the studio of the Venetian master, Giovanni Domenico Tiepolo, who painted her portrait against a hazy silhouette of our city in 1793. Though her name has been forgotten, my ancestor will always be remembered by the artwork that conveys the intelligence and good nature of the greyhound, as well as the artist's great affection for our breed. Late in life, Gian Domenico painted the simple masterpiece for Villa Zianigo, his summer house on the mainland, which now hangs in a palazzo on the Grand Canal that once housed rich and powerful families but today holds only their aging furniture and works of art.

When I was a pup, my mother often took me to Ca'Rezzonico to view this portrait. As through the cool galleries we moved side by side, she spoke in hushed tones of her own upbringing. With sadness in her voice, she recounted how the early comforts of her home abruptly ended when her father, a Roman racing dog of superior strength and legendary speed, was injured. His leg broken, my grandfather—though a great athlete who had brought both honor and profit to his owners— was cruelly put down by his trainer. Is it any wonder that to the present day we Fortunatos resist the collar and disdain even the thought of servitude to any master? Of this my mother reminded me every time she recalled the murder that forced my grandmother to divide her family to live with various relatives.

Moving in with an elderly aunt of limited means in San Polo, Isabella was sent out at a young age to beg in the Mercato di Rialto. One morning while she sat with sad eyes by the steps of the arched bridge, my father first noticed this statuesque beauty on his way to the *Pescaria* to purchase oysters from the lagoon for his midday meal.

Day by day she was charmed by the short-legged artist in the pork pie hat who presented her with small bags of biscuits—some filled with jam, others flavored with anise, and the ones he soon discovered were her favorite, the *biscotti di regina* studded with the pale seeds of the sesame plant. By the end of that mild summer, despite her aunt's objections, they were wed in la Chiesa di San Felice, a small church a short distance from the house where I was raised.

Isabella too was an artist, and as a pup I used to sit by her paws on our balcony overlooking the canal. There I watched her paint with much delicacy and detail our *sestiere*—a district bustling with workmen, shopkeepers and vendors with their icy crates of sardines, baskets of crabs and bulbs of bright green fennel. When Mama painted, it came to life—the purple radicchio with its curling white veins, the overlapping movements of the boats, barges and people walking along the quay—the light as it filtered through the outstretched wing of a dove. She could even paint the coolness of the evening as it spread like a shadow over the canal.

In my father's studio I learned to love the clang of steel, the fizzling spray of sparks from his welder, the smell of burning metal and the underlying rumble of the compressor that accompanied the air hammer and chisel as he sculpted. But in the stillness that surrounded my mother as she painted, I learned the quiet between each moment of creation.

And so I learned the ways of the artist—an education that led us every Saturday to the Gallerie dell'Accademia. Here at the museum my mother sketched the angels, saints, Madonnas, and the occasional hound in the paintings of the Venetian masters. Her favorite was Tintoretto.

When this great artist was a boy working in the shop where his father dyed cloth, he first drew with charcoal on the walls. My mother often reminded me how without going to school, the young genius learned his lessons from looking very closely at the great art of Venice. This story was intended as a nudge for me to pay attention to the framed wonders around us. She disapproved of my obsession that summer with Tintin whose adventures, immortalized in the comics of Hergé, lay open before me on the marble floor where I lounged in the Renaissance room reading at her paws.

Even in Rome when we visited the Vatican, Tintin and his

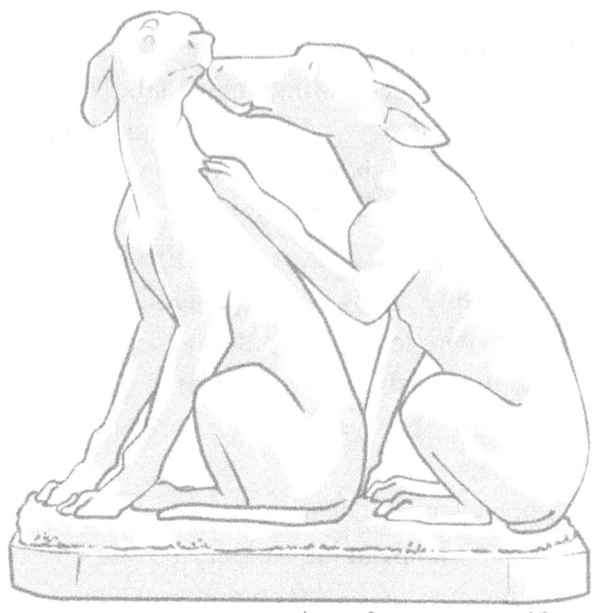

artist unknown Rome circa 1st century C.E

friend, an admirable canine called Snowy, occupied my thoughts—which only once were drawn in by an ancient work of art. It was a marble sculpture of two seated greyhounds that the tour guide said were at play.

But looking up from the pages of *Tintin in Tibet*, I disagreed. All eyes turned to me, and I said that they were not playing at all, but that one was healing the other, licking his wounded ear. The tour guide glared at me for the interruption and then raised her flag for us to follow, but my mother smiled and whispered, "Good point, Piccolo, but their kind will rarely admit that."

One day while my mother was mixing gesso and water in a glass bowl, my father came to her and gently nuzzled her neck beneath her rosebud ear. "Isabella," he said softly. "I am going to America."

"Alfonso," she whimpered, licking his blue-black muzzle with deep affection. "The voyage is long and the dangers in that distant land are many. I beg you. Stay here with us in Venezia."

But my father's dream had always been to try his luck in the City of York they call New and having studied English late into the night and often practicing on tourists, he felt ready to make his move. And though he came of a diminutive breed, his father had trained him in physical culture just as Papa trained me from eight weeks old, strengthening us to withstand the hardships of independent living and ply our various trades.

Born of an ancestral line of hunters known for our endurance, we Fortunatos have always been quick to pick up the scent of adventure and take up the challenge of a chase.

Looking back on my own life, I understand that Alfonso could not resist the urge of his bloodline. Yet still I feel the sadness of a pup when I recall those events that now unfold before my eyes as if they are happening in the present moment.

My mother and I watch him pack his leather satchel with his sculpting tools—the chisels, mallets, gouges, hammers, files, a grinder and his torch. Sadly, we follow him to the corner of the studio where on a low sofa beneath a tall lamp each night, he and Mama used to sit, reading and discussing both classic and contemporary authors.

Papa runs his paw along the smooth surface of the shelf cut from a hardwood plank that we sanded together before brushing on the many thin coats of tung oil into its swirling grain.

"Take good care of these," he says of our books which include his vintage first edition titles of the Modern Library, many still wrapped in their dust jackets. He nods toward the twenty-three titles of the Tintin series that they have collected over the years. Their covers show more signs of wear from having been read to me nightly as a pup.

"And these." Papa nods toward his collection of Blue Note records and vintage albums of Frank Sinatra, Ella Fitzgerald and Tony Bennett. My papa's voice resembles that of the great singer of New York—whose own father, born in Calabria, had long ago packed a suitcase and prepared for this same journey. He like

Alfonso must have had to find a way to say good-bye. Now from the pale blue cover of the oldest album in his collection, my father takes a record from its sleeve and places it on the turntable and sings with all his heart.

The song is *Because of You*, and Isabella joins him—the warmth of her voice enveloping each note as she holds her short-legged husband close, dipping and spinning him around the living room.

I nod and try to smile but as happens with my species, I sneeze with great emotion when the time draws near for his ship to depart. Then from the nail above the shelf Papa takes his pork pie hat.

Mama whimpers though he tries to reassure her. "Biscotti," he says, for this is his sweet name for her. "My Biscotti, don't cry. For as soon as I make my fortune, I will send for you and the bambino."

But sad to say that letter never comes. For over two years we wait, making our living selling mama's smaller works, mostly watercolors and pastels, to the tourists who flock to the Piazza di San Marco—each morning pulling our cart to the square where she displays her work and sets up her easel to paint throughout the day.

At noon she gives me two euros to run to one of the many crowded eateries. I nose my way through the crowd of locals and tourists who have gathered at the counter to order *cicchetti,* the savory bites prepared from whatever is fresh each morning in the market. My favorite are the small plates of *crostini*—fried pieces of bread topped with paper-thin prosciutto or the creamed salt cod that tickles my nostrils.

One day it is so difficult to choose that Mama becomes worried in my absence and leaves her place in the square, only to find me with two paws on the glass display case, my eyes wide, transfixed by the abundance. From the doorway she barks, snapping me out of my daze before nosing her way through the crowd to the counter. Pointing with a flick of her head, she selects *sarde in saor,* sardines in a sweet-sour onion sauce, and *polpette*, the fried meatballs which were my father's favorite—a snack he always washed down with a splash of wine poured into his bowl from the porcelain jug.

Sitting at a small table—a privilege for which tourists have to pay but for us is free as Alfonso used to be great friends with the owner of this *bàcaro*—and after licking the last crumb from my plate, I tell her what is in my heart. "Mama, I am a big dog now, and the time has come for me to go to America to look for Papa."

"But, my Piccolo," she whines. "What if you do not find him? What will you do in that big country that swallowed him up without even a word for his family? I fear that place, Piccolo. America she is hungry and will swallow you up like your papa." Isabella bows her head, and her ears quiver as she sniffles.

"Mama, don't worry. I have a good set of paws to work and a nose to match. Believe me, Mama. I will find Papa."

"But what if you don't? What if this America, she gobbles you up as she gobbled up my Alfonso?"

"Don't worry, Mama. I promise to find Papa, and fortune as an artist in America."

Within days of my decision, she watches with grief as I prepare for my journey. In a canvas bag I place my portfolio thick with photographs of my many sculptures and drawings of those I will one day make. While I am packing, Mama leaves the dim room where we sleep and passes under the blanket that hangs from the ceiling. You see, dear reader, ever since my father's departure our life has become difficult, and we have given up the duplex apartment that had been both home and studio in Cannaregio for a more affordable ground floor room. Here the constant dampness causes us both sinus problems throughout the fall and winter.

From the corner where we keep her easel and our cart, Mama brings a blue bag of biscotti that she sets down beside my duffel bag, a gift for me her only son on his voyage to America.

With the last of our savings Mama has paid for my passage on a ship called *Preziosa*. At noon on that spring day, we hurry to the pier to catch the *vaparetto,* the water taxi that will take us to San Basilio, the slip from which she will sail. As *la Marangona* tolls from the bell tower of my beloved piazza, my tail sags motionless behind me.

After I board the ship, my mother stands on the promenade and howls with the sadness of our parting as the last thin line of land fades in the distance.

I then drag my duffel bag to my cabin where I climb onto my mattress and circle several times before pawing the blanket and falling into a troubled sleep.

But being a young dog on his first adventure, when the morning light spills over my porthole, I leap from my bed and out the door. Up the iron stairs I bolt, my nostrils flare, inhaling all the smells that wash over me on waves of salty air. Every deck, every railing, the entire ship from bow to stern, happily I sniff. My ears alert, I listen avidly to all the conversations that flow around me. One evening in the dining room, I overhear the passengers at my table speak of a famous American artist.

"Excuse me? But who is this famous artist, and how might I meet him?"

They tell me his name is Guy Gizárd, an American artist of international fame and although he is rarely sighted in the dining room or other common areas of the ship, he is known to walk the uppermost deck at dawn.

So thrilled am I at the thought of meeting a real American artist that I do not sleep in my bed that night, choosing instead to curl up on a lounge chair near the spot where he has been sighted. I bring along a small wool blanket which I pull over my frosty nostrils to await the sunrise and the appearance of Guy Gizárd. I imagine that being a great artist, Mr. Gizárd must awaken so early to study the effects of light on the open sea. Eager to join him in his study of nature, I wait throughout that tail-chilling night.

But just before dawn, heaviness overtakes my eyes while on the briny air I smell Mama's risotto simmering in the black ink of the squid. Stretching before me, the Piazza is silent and empty at dawn when in the distance I hear the wooden wheels of our cart on the slabs of stone that pave the square where my mother now approaches, pulling it alone.

"Piccolo, Piccolo," she calls to me, and with my paws twitching in my sleep I race to meet her.

But then from her slender back sprout two white-tipped grey wings. Flying to the pier from which my ship had sailed, she lands on a barnacle encrusted piling where she cranes her neck and squawks raucously as a splash of icy water awakes me from my dream to see a noisy seagull perched on the railing of the *Preziosa.*

Sitting up, I watch the star-filled night grow faint along the horizon where a long stroke of pale orange and another of violet separate the sea and sky, and my old life in Venice from the strange events that are soon to follow.

Against that backdrop, I see the silhouette of a short stout man who wears a long leather coat and leans over the rail. When he straightens up and turns around, he is dabbing his mouth with a handkerchief. His scrawny legs are bare beneath his coat, and on his feet he wears the same white slippers I have seen on other passengers.

Tossing off the blanket, I approach the man who looks pale and ill. "Are you alright?"

"Nothing wrong with me that a little hair of the dog can't fix." He takes a silver flask from his inside pocket, unscrews the cap and tips back his head to drain the contents.

"What dog?"

"As in hung over?"

"Hung over what?"

"You know, like an eighteen-wheeler slammed into your brain after you put down a few too many."

"Put down?" I repeat the dreaded phrase.

"You don't drink, do you?"

"Only water, and on special occasions a little wine with Mama and Papa."

"How old are you, kid?"

"Three."

"No wonder, you're just a baby."

"Baby? I am a full-grown Italian greyhound of an old and honored family, the Fortunatos of Venice. And I am going to America to find my father."

"Fortunato, huh? Son of Fortunato."

"You know my papa?" I bark. And unable to contain my excitement, I jump with my front paws landing squarely on the stranger's chest.

"Down, get down!" He stumbles backward, grasping the ship's rail. "This coat is worth more than your life."

I fall onto my haunches and feel a pang of shame at having so abandoned all control in front of the stranger. My ears tilting downward, I apologize profusely, and showing the ultimate sign for sorry, I roll on my back and allow the man to rub my belly.

"No problem, kid. But to answer your question no, I don't know your dad, but I have heard of the Fortunato family. Who hasn't?"

My chest swells with pride to think that our name is known beyond the narrow streets of our neighborhood, and I give my paw to the man who shakes it in his hand.

"I am Piccolo Fortunato. And you, sir? Are you Guy Gizárd the famous American artist?"

"The most famous," he replies with a belch.

"Please, Mr. Gizárd, I too am an artist. And I am very interested in the town called Soho in your country."

"Soho, kid? What've you been living in a cave? It's all happening in Chelsea. Has been since the 90s."

I dip my head submissively. "No, I was not living in a cave but in the back room of a ground floor apartment near the *Canalosso* which Mama rents for ten euros a week."

"Ground floor? When that *acqua alta* hits, you're like, what?

Three feet underwater."

"Yes, indeed, sir. Many times we have been in the Piazza when the sirens sound and water rises between the paving stones. Then we pack our cart and hurry home to carry the few belongings we have not sold along with Mama's paintings up the stairs to join our neighbors on the second floor to wait for the waters to recede. We are accustomed to this. But it is the dampness in the nostrils which is a hardship. And the fact that due to poor wiring, in the evening it is difficult to read. Yet it is where we have had to live while we await the return of my father."

"Don't worry about it, kid. Life's got its ups and down, maybe you're due for a change of fortune, eh, Fortunato?"

It is not the first time I have heard this joke, but I bare my teeth slightly as I have come to understand is an acknowledgment of humor. Guy Gizárd scratches me behind my ear, and I stand beside him at the railing watching the shifting colors give way to a cool white sun on the horizon.

"That's better, kid. So, let me guess, you're an artist, huh? Got a portfolio?"

"Yes, I do, and in it over a hundred photographs of my sculptures and drawings for a hundred more."

"Then, young Fortunato, meet me in the dining room at midnight for a nightcap. How's that for starters?"

"For starters that is excellent." My tail wags lashing Guy Gizárd's bare leg. "But as I do not have a night cap, I will wear my welding cap, thank you."

"Don't mention it, kid, I'm always looking out for the underdog. It's just my nature."

"You are a very kind man."

"Whatever. Just be there by twelve, and we'll toss back some Jack Daniels."

"Excuse me, but who is this Jack, and why would we—how do you say, toss him back?"

"Jack's a real American, and tonight I'll introduce you."

"Thank you, Mr. Gizárd." I bark before running to my cabin to review my portfolio and consider how best I might present my work that night.

I sense that this man Guy Gizárd is about to change the course of my life, so I scrub my yellow welding cap in the sink, and with the metal file from my tool roll I clean the rough edges from my nails, then with a length of thread I floss between my teeth.

The hours drag throughout that sunless day as I pad back and forth on the decks. The misty evening gives way to a drizzly night, and at twelve o'clock I enter the dining room and ask the waiter to seat me at the table of Guy Gizárd. Proudly I set down my portfolio before him and watch with nervous anticipation. As I observe that Mr. Gizárd has in fact not worn his night cap, I remove my welding cap and place it on the table.

"Alright, kid, let's see what you got." He opens my portfolio and flips past the images of my marble, wood and stone carvings as well as the assemblages of steel I have made in my father's studio. My heart races and my stomach feels queasy. At first, I want to take my book and run from the room thinking with shame that he does not like my work. Then when he tosses my portfolio carelessly aside, I feel a growl rising in my throat at the disrespect.

Fortunately, Mama has taught me to think before I speak, and so when the great artist nods approvingly, I am glad I have not shown my anger.

"Nice work. You really seem to know your stuff. But, kid, you're all over the place, you've got to focus."

"I don't understand, Mr. Gizárd, is it not good for an artist to master many methods and styles?"

"It's all about the brand, always has been. Collectors want to know what they're getting, and I'm telling you, kid, stick with the steelwork. You got potential, but it's got to go in one direction if you want to get ahead."

"I see," I say even though I can't really understand, being disoriented by the newness of my surroundings and his unusual advice as Papa has always taught me to be a master of all materials. He tips back a glass filled with amber liquid.

"So, what's the plan?"

"I have only two. To do my artwork and to find my papa."

"Let me guess. He took off to America to find fame and fortune and never came home."

"Yes, exactly, but how do you know this?"

"Let's just say I know the artistic temperament."

"Again, you are correct. My papa, he is a true artist."

"No doubt, kid. But just remember, America's a big place—and New York City's even bigger. Take just about any street in Manhattan, and there's more distraction than you can shake a stick at. A young artist gets here with one intention, but a thousand temptations pull him in that many directions. There's something for every appetite, and once you've fed one, there's another taste you want to try."

Out of respect I remain quiet, but in my jaws I feel a quiver, the urge to bite the man who has insulted my father's good character—for Papa would never have strayed from his commitment to make art and return to his beloved Biscotti.

"But appetites and rent take money. How much you got on you?"

"Fifty-seven euros."

"In New York City, kid, that's *bupkis*."

"Bupkis?"

"Like barely enough for a decent meal. And when you got bupkis in New York, kid, you're nobody. And when you're nobody, that's when the trouble starts."

"What kind of trouble, Mr. Gizárd?"

"All sorts of trouble, bill collectors, city marshals throwing you out of your place. Shelters, soup kitchens, cops harassing you." He nods at me as if I might be in such danger.

"I have never lived on the streets."

"Lots of loners end up there. So, before you go looking for

your papa, you need to get yourself set up. Make some connections, meet the kind of people who can help get you to the money."

"But I don't know anyone in America. How will I meet these people?"

"Well, you're off to a good start, kid, because right now I'm about to introduce you to that friend of mine."

In the corner seated on a stool at the bar, a young man in a white jacket has started to doze off. Mr. Gizárd snaps his fingers, startling him awake. "Bus boy, bring me a bowl for my friend here."

To be called friend by such a great and powerful man, I feel proud and sit up even straighter in my chair.

Before me, the busboy sets down a porcelain bowl with a golden edge. Mr. Gizárd reaches across the table, and I watch his thick hand tilt the square bottle with a black and white label, pouring the pale liquid into my dish.

"But where is your friend, Mr. Gizárd? Will he be joining us?" I scan the dining room, empty except for the busboy who is stripping the dirty linen from the other tables.

"He's right there in front of you, kid. Jack Daniels, a real eighty-proof, blue-blooded American. Go ahead lap it up."

Its smell offends me, and I do not wish to drink. But wanting to please my host, I outstretch my tongue and try to take in a sip—but the muscles in my jaws tighten as I pull back my head and shake it in disgust.

"Don't worry, the next one'll go down easier, always does." Guy Gizárd refills his own glass. "So, you want to be an artist in New York?"

"Very much, Mr. Gizárd."

"Stick with me, kid, and your work will be all over. Galleries, museums, you name it. But you have to follow my lead. First order of business, let's see you make my friend Jack disappear."

With much apprehension, I set my paws on either side of the

bowl, lean forward and plunge my tongue into the foul-smelling liquid. A single gulp runs its course down my gullet like flaming oil, blurring my vision and making every muscle in my body clench. I push the bowl onto the carpet. Swaying, I try to focus on the many images of the great American artist whose words echo across the table.

"Really packs a wallop, don't it?" He laughs with a snort.

I nod at the many faces of Guy Gizárd, watching his many hands draw many briefcases from the floor and set them on the table. Then his many fingers remove from them what appears to be countless pages.

My tongue feels thick, and my words are slurred. "What are those?"

"Your ticket to fame and fortune in America. Sign this contract and I will set you up in your own studio, kid, where you can turn those sketches into sculpture."

"But why?"

"Let's just say I love good art." On the table he places the white pages before me. "Just make your mark here, and I swear those steel pieces will not only be in the Gallstone Gallery but stick with me, and your work will be in the next Gauntley Biennial."

Although the room is spinning, and for every busboy I see three, those words ring clearly in my ears—my work in the next Gauntley Biennial. I offer no resistance when Guy Gizárd takes a small metal tin from the pocket of his robe and flips it open. He grasps my paw, pressing it onto the ink pad then onto the contract to make my mark, the pawprint of the Fortunatos of Venice. Again, he reaches for the dreaded bottle to refill his glass and picking up the bowl from the floor, he fills it to the brim.

"Now we won't consider our deal sealed until we drink a toast."

I place my paws on the table but feel nothing beneath them. I swerve, leaning forward, aiming my muzzle at the amber pool, but miss and losing my balance fall headfirst to the floor. There throughout that night, alone I lie on the whisky sodden carpet that fouls my dreams with its sour stench.

My head pounding, I awake the next morning with the leather boot of Mr. Guy Gizárd jabbing me in the ribs.

"C'mon, kid. Time to get up and get going."

Dazed, I rise and follow him to the deck where the harsh light blazing off the water hurts my eyes. Dimly I recall the night before. "My portfolio. I must retrieve it from the dining room."

"Don't worry, kid, I got it." He snaps a leash onto my collar and leads me down the gangplank into the mob that has gathered to greet the passengers of the *Preziosa*.

A leash. I yank at the chain that tautens between us.

"Calm down," says Guy Gizárd, pulling me along by his side as he strides down the pier. "It's just a formality. It'll come off as soon as we get to the studio. Besides, this is New York City, and I wouldn't want you to get lost."

Gizárd leads me to a parking lot where a semi-bald man in a blue blazer waits. The sunlight glints off the tiny gold cross that dangles from his ear, and his overly sweet smell makes my nose twitch and my stomach churn.

"Mason, this is the one I was telling you about. Kid, Mason Maldonado, my assistant."

Handed the leash, the man yanks forcefully. I snarl and snap at his manicured fingertips.

"Don't worry, Mason. This one's all bark and no bite." He dips down behind the door of a sleek silver car held open for him by his driver. "And Mason, give it a break with the Givenchy knock-off. I could smell you from the boat."

"What do you mean, knock off? I bought it outside Macy's."

"Whatever, just take the dog back to Brooklyn, and I'll be by in a couple weeks to check on him."

"But where are you going?" I ask with my head hurting even more from the movement of my jaws. "I thought I was going with you to the town of Chelsea?"

"Relax, kid, you'll get there. But first you've got to make the work, right? South Street," he says to the driver who closes the rear door and moves around to the front seat.

I scratch at the car door confused why after all we discussed, he is leaving me on the end of a chain held by this man, Mason Maldonado. "I don't understand."

The tinted window rolls down. "Hey, watch the paint," Gizárd growls. I sit down on the gravel of the parking lot and though I try to control them, three whimpers rise from my throat.

"Alright, alright, don't worry. Just go with Mason, and he'll set you up, okay? You'll have the studio all to yourself, and you can start knocking out that steel work you showed me last night. And, Mason, keep an eye on this one." Then the dark window glides up and the Lexus pulls out of the lot, turning into the flow of southbound traffic.

"C'mon, you heard the boss." Gizárd's assistant tugs on the leash. "You got work to do."

He pulls me through the crowd. My head bowed in shame, I follow at the end of the chain that binds me to his thick-fingered hand, studded with rings and a fat wrist encircled with gold bracelets.

At the edge of the parking lot, he opens the door of a white jeep. "Go on, jump."

With the smell of leather overtaking the heavy scent of his cologne, I leap onto the backseat where he sets down my leash before walking around to the driver's side of the vehicle. For a moment my haze lifts and I think to myself, "Run, Piccolo, run!" But it is another voice in my head that holds me back, the voice of Guy Gizárd whispering his promise from our meeting the previous night. "Stick with me, kid, and your work will be in the next Gauntley Biennial."

And as the key turns in the ignition and the engine hums, I shift my attention to the city beyond the dashboard. Riding through the streets of New York with the window rolled down, I forget my distress.

From the many restaurants waft the scents of foods I can't identify but that make my mouth water, and on every corner the smell of meat grilling rises from the stainless-steel carts of vendors.

"Yo," he snaps glancing up into the rear-view mirror. "You hungry? Want a hot dog or something?"

"A hot dog?"

"Don't worry, it's not what you're thinking. A frankfurter, you know, like a sausage."

I distrust this man, Mason Maldonado, but the suggestion of meat sounds so appealing that although I try to control them, my tongue rolls from my mouth and my long tail beats against the door as he pulls the jeep up to the curb.

"Yo, gimme one with the works."

I watch the whitish-gloved hand raise a hatch and dip down a pair of tongs into the steaming well. It rests the hot dog onto a pillowy white roll, and then from glass canisters scoops out chopped onions and relish, spreading them over the long meat that peeks out from between the split halves of the bun. Mason hands the man two bills that he tucks into the pocket of his stained apron.

Pulling away from the curb with one hand on the leather-bound wheel, Mason turns slightly to hand me the hotdog over his shoulder. Instantly the mingled smells of savory meat and sweet tomatoes revive my senses. I bite down past the fluffy bread and into the casing of the frankfurter that snaps, releasing the oil, heat and spices into my mouth.

"Not bad, huh?"

I nod, my mouth too full of this flavorful new snack to speak. Looking over the river as we cruise across the Williamsburg Bridge, I observe the sun on the water that glints like shards of glass, dividing the skyscrapers behind us from the approaching patchwork of rooftops and water towers.

Licking the last speck of relish from my paw, I stretch my

neck and peer out the window, hoping to catch a glimpse of the once famous town of which my father so often spoke. "Which way is Soho?"

"Manhattan, that's where we just came from. And that's Brooklyn coming up ahead. And down there, that's the East River, about as clean as those canals you got back in your hometown."

"You have been to my city?"

"Me, Venice? Plenty of times. In fact, the first trip in my life was when Guy took me with him to set up the Biennial back in 80."

His gaze fixed on the traffic light, he is silent as it seems to me his mind has wandered back and is sniffing around the yard of some distant place. The light turns green and with a shrug of his shoulders, he shakes off the reverie. "But that was long before you showed up in the Piazza, huh?"

"Yes, I work there with my mother, but how do you know?"

"I, uh, know from Guy," Mason falters. "Yeah, he mentioned he met an artist from, yeah, Venice and that he wanted to set you up in the studio in Brooklyn for a while. Just long enough so you could get some work done."

"Is Mr. Gizárd always so generous with young artists?"

"Listen, dog boy, I think I had enough questions for one day."

Mason slows down on a street where from an open fire hydrant a blast of water arcs over a plank of wood that two boys hold against the pounding stream. With a push of a button Mason raises the windows as he drives through the deluge, then turns to look me straight in the eye. "And when something's free, you just take it and don't ask any questions. Got it?"

We drive on past long avenues of storefronts armored by steel doors and vacant lots surrounded by fences crowned with curling razor wire. I sit silently with my nose out the half-open window and my ears tilting back in the breeze. Mason turns down a narrow avenue crowded with shops and sidewalk cafes, then leans heavily on his horn.

"Double parkers. Can't even drive around here anymore. Used to be beautiful, like a no-man's land. Now look at it."

I do look, and what I see I admire. Many good-looking young people, sleek and long legged who roam the street, some sitting on steps and others at outdoor cafes. They seem to me to be a thirsty breed as most of them carry a bottle of water or a tall, steaming cup. A female whose septum is pierced with a thin silver bar points toward me, her forearm laced with blue branches and birds.

"Check out the greyhound," she says to her attractive companion whose dark eyes widen when I reply *ciao, bella*—smiling as we drive past.

Mason gives me a wink in the rear-view mirror. "Yo, dog, I see you like the ladies."

"Yes, I admire them greatly," I reply with a sigh.

When we come to Morgan Avenue, Mason veers left and then pulls up to a steel roll gate where a tall boy in a hooded sweatshirt kneels shaking a can of paint that he points toward the bricks.

"Paint one stroke on that wall, kid, and you're gonna lick it off," he shouts out the window at the boy who grabs the board with wheels, throws it on the sidewalk and takes off down the block.

"Kids. Got no respect for other people's property."

His bracelets clinking against the dashboard, he reaches into the glove compartment for a small device on which he presses his thumb, raising the gate through which we drive into the courtyard of what appears to be a silent factory. From somewhere inside, I hear the muffled bark of a dog and catch the scent of a rodent. Turning in the direction of its squeak, I see a rat squeeze through a crack between a basement window frame and the crumbling sill, scurry across the cement, up the side of an open dumpster and dive into the garbage.

"Come on, dog boy. We'll take the freight elevator up."

Inside the building a single yellow bulb casts a dim light down the hallway where Mason unbolts a heavy door. I follow at his heels into the dusty elevator where he tugs on a steel cable and the elevator clanks, taking us slowly upward.

He leads me out onto the fourth floor. "This is it. Your new home."

Whatever doubts have assailed me since I left the ship, fly out the open windows of the spacious studio where Mason unclasps the chain from my collar. It is a wide industrial space with a tin ceiling supported by columns. Down the length of the studio runs a yellow rail from which a hoist is suspended.

"An overhead crane." I marvel at the mechanism as Mason takes hold of the controls that hang from the ceiling on a chord. Pushing the button which brings the hoist to us, he lowers the black iron hook.

"Go ahead, dog boy, go for it." I leap up to grab hold and Mason raises me halfway to the ceiling and then takes me for a ride across the studio.

"Even a little guy like you could do a lot with a toy like this, huh?"

Being full-grown, I am offended by his use of the words little and toy—but thrilled by my new surroundings where through the open windows wafts the aroma of various meats. I sniff the air to distinguish the intertwining smells.

"Salami, ham." I sniff again. "A cold cut of beef?"

"Yeah, you got some nose. That's from Boar's Head over on Rock Street."

I sniff more deeply.

"And in the distance, I smell foul water without movement, a smell of diesel and rotting meat combined."

"Oh yo, that's gotta be the Gowanus, but that's like a few miles from here."

"After all, I am a dog and though limited in range of color, we are gifted with a sense of smell far beyond your ability." I move toward the open window and sniff again. "And closer to this domicile, a highly attractive female of your species is passing."

Mason moves to the sill and leans out, looking up and down

the street, then waves.

"Yo, Lola, what's up?"

A pleasant voice rises to the window. "Not much, and you?"

"Same old, same old. Tell your brother I said come by."

"Yeah, whatever."

I lean over the sill and admire the sight of the female whose long lean legs so like a greyhound's extend from her short white pants, elevated by the thin, long heels of her shoes. As she approaches a car that pulls up to the curb and leans into the open window on the passenger side, I feel envious of the driver to have the attention of so lovely a creature.

"Yeah, that's pretty amazing how you take all that in through your nose."

"Amazing to you, perhaps, but essential to my survival and as a source of my artwork."

"So yo, Sniff, what do you think of the digs?"

"Digs?" I suddenly am overcome with a desire to unearth and gnaw a bone.

"As in place to live?"

"Oh, yes, a perfect place to sleep and work. And what of you, how long have you lived here?"

"Me? Since I'm like sixteen, seventeen, Guy's been here maybe over twenty. He bought it back in the eighties when it was still dirt cheap."

"It is a fine space for any artist."

"Used to be a factory. You can see stains from where the machine oil leaked on the floor." Under my paws I admire the wide maple slats that long ago had been burnished beneath the soles of workers' boots. "You got any idea what a space like this would cost these days?"

I shake my head.

"Five thousand square feet? Cut up into cubicles for these hipsters? Six, eight grand a month easy. Multiply that by three floors, and you're talking *buku* bucks."

"And it all belongs to Mr. Gizárd?"

"For a couple years he just rented a space in the basement from some Hassid. But when his work started to sell, Guy bought it from him for like a hundred grand. Now? It's worth a couple mill easy."

"Mill?"

"As in seven figures," he says without clarifying my confusion. "But to tell you the truth, I think he was happier when he first showed up on the block. Back then, he'd get up around noon, and us kids would come by and watch him work. Later around five, six o'clock, we'd walk him to the bodega where he'd buy himself a six-pack of Bud, Sunny-D and chips for us. Yeah, back in the day."

"Does he still work here?"

"Not much. He's got a place on South Street right on the water. This building is well, sort of for guests."

"And do you sleep in this building?"

"Yeah, I got a space on the ground floor. I been with Guy now, like I said for over twenty years. He's always looked out for me, and I look out for him."

I follow Mason across the loft, my nails tapping on the hardwood floor to an area with steel shelving units, neatly stacked with tools and containers of supplies: boxes of charcoal, rolls of paper, grinders, chisels, blades, a circular saw. Then on a nearby workbench I see my portfolio and the blue bag from the biscotti which now contains only crumbs. The duffel bag with my torch hangs from a nail on the wall, and there beside my welding cap is my leather tool roll.

"Guy had your stuff sent over."

Carefully I untie the roll with my teeth "This was my father's first set of carving tools. He made the handles himself."

"Well, from what Guy told me, you're not gonna be doing any carving. He wants you working on steel and only steel. In fact, he called this morning. Sent me to a welding supply place way the hell out in East New York to pick this up." Mason drags a cardboard box by its flap from the corner. "He said you couldn't cut through tin foil with that toy torch of yours."

"A plasma arc cutter." I read the side of the box as my tail is beating against a leg of the workbench. "Hobart Air Force 700i."

"Yeah, the real deal, it'll cut up to seven eighths of stainless. Guy says that'll be plenty for you."

"Yes, it, it is a very powerful tool." I stutter overwhelmed by the magnitude of the gift.

"Well, you gotta get cracking, dog boy. Biennial's in a couple months."

"Cracking? I don't understand this cracking."

"Cracking, you know, get started."

"Yes, I will. I will get started right away."

"In that room there, you got all your materials. Check it out."

Peering into the adjoining room stocked with plates of stainless steel and chunks of stone, I see the trunk of a once magnificent tree that by its smell I know is cherry. Then I run my paw over the surface of a cool slab of marble, admiring the rich gold veins that stream through the brilliant black stone.

"Portoro. This stone was quarried in the province of La Spezia."

"Yeah, well, I see you know your stuff, dog boy."

"Yes, my father, he spent many hours with me in the basilicas and palazzi of our city, teaching me about the materials and techniques used by the artisans who built them."

"Yeah, your old man's pretty smart. And I see you take after him."

I bow my head and in return for the compliment allow him to scratch behind my ear.

"Yeah, cost Guy an arm and leg, but he's never gonna use it. Like that hunk of wood. Another waste of money. You don't know what it took to get it down here from Guy's property in the Adirondacks. But that's Guy, he sees it, he wants it, he brings it

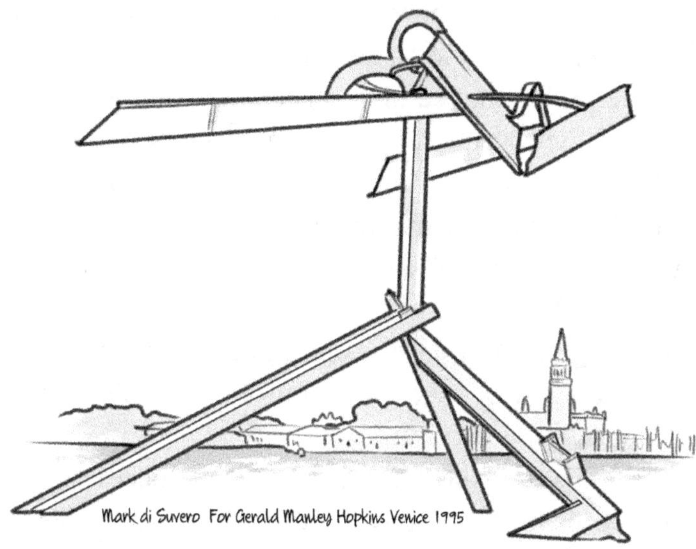

back. Took three guys with a crane truck, two days to take out the window and get it up here."

Although most of the bark has already been stripped from the tree, a slender branch with three small leaves extends from the trunk. I take it in my mouth and chew on it with my back teeth.

"Yeah, he was planning to do some woodwork, but Gloria put the kibosh on that real fast. Steel and only steel she told him and that was that."

"And who is this Gloria?" I take a small leaf between my front teeth and pull it off the limb.

"Gloria Gallstone, she's got a gallery in Chelsea, strictly blue chip. Guy first started showing with Galoshian, but then he and Harry had a falling out."

"Falling out of what?"

"As in couldn't see eye to eye—Harry had all the big names like Serra and di Suvero. And long story short, Guy didn't like playing second fiddle."

"Yes, I have heard of this man di Suvero." And although I do not understand his talk of fiddles, my father had been greatly inspired by this artist whose bright and towering sculptures were exhibited along the Grand Canal when he was a young dog. And it was that poetry that moved him to become a sculptor.

"Yeah, I met him a couple of times. Good guy. Put his heart and soul into the work. Made it himself—not like a lot of these losers. But I couldn't say that to Guy."

"What do you mean? Made it himself? Do not all artists make their own work?"

"Yeah, right. So anyway, back in the 90s when Gloria moved from Soho to Chelsea, she took him on. Now she's the one who calls the shots."

"Shots?" I say, cringing at the thought of needles.

"Not those shots, dog boy, you know, calls the shots, the ways things gotta go. She gets the clients hungry, and Guy brings in the meat."

I do not fully understand Mason, but in this city, I have much to learn. "This wood, she is so beautiful, and I can see by its width well over a hundred years old."

"Well, it might as well be sitting here for another hundred. Guy's got no use for it."

"I would be happy to sculpt from it a piece for Mr. Gizárd. To show my thanks."

"Yeah, well, don't worry about it. Just stick with the metal—like Guy said, steel and only steel, *capiche*?"

I tilt my head and for a moment study this stranger who has uttered a word in my native tongue.

"Hey, what? A *goombah* from Bensonhurst can't speak the mother tongue?"

"I am surprised."

"Don't be. I got it from my mother, who got it from her mother who came to Brooklyn via Calabria." I look at this man differently now, not as a stranger but a countryman.

"And what about you? An Italian greyhound who speaks like

perfect English? What's that about?"

"It had always been my father's dream to come to America, and so he spoke often with the tourists and studied English late into the night, so that when his time came, he would be ready."

"So, your Pops can read?"

"Oh, yes. But he not only studied English from the book. He loved American music—your big bands, blues, jazz, and often he would sing the songs of Frank Sinatra to my mother."

"Nice."

"And American film. My papa very much admired the movies of Sylvester Stallone."

"Another goombah."

"I remember one Saturday when I was a pup, he came home from the *Mercatino di San Giobbe* with a full boxset of the Rocky videos which we watched together many nights. He also brought home *Rambo First Blood* part one and two, but my mother disapproved of my viewing them. Although several times when she traveled to Naples to see her sister, we did watch them together."

"That's one way to learn English.

"My Papa's English, it is excellent."

"He didn't do a bad job teaching you."

"Whatever knowledge that my father had, he made sure to teach… to me." Dipping my head, I avert Mason's eyes, but he gets down on one knee and pats my chest.

"Hey, you okay, dog boy? Listen, what I learned in life is if you don't think about it too much, it don't hurt so bad. So, don't think about it."

What he has suggested is not possible, but I give my tail a single wag to show appreciation for his attempt to counsel me.

"Okay, that's better." Mason gets up with some difficulty due to his bloated abdomen. "I'll be back later with your grub."

"Grub?"

"Grub, as in nose bag, food?"

"Oh, my meals. Mama always made them for me."

"Yeah, well, I'm actually pretty good myself. I've been cooking for Guy for years. He tends to like it hot, but for you I'll go easy on the Sriracha."

"Sriracha?"

"You know, the sauce—like heavy on the garlic, heavier on the hot."

"Do you speak of the peperoncini?"

"And then some. They don't grow hot enough for Guy. Come here." He snaps his fingers and leads me past a small, well-equipped kitchen to a side room where behind a heavy sheet of plastic, sun lamps raise the temperature to a high degree of warmth that makes me pant. I scan the long table lined with earthen pots filled with dirt where tiny peppers poke out from under green leaves. Mason reaches for a water bottle and grasping and releasing the handle, he sprays a veil of mist over the plants.

"You got your jalapeños, serranoes, we even got a couple Carolina Reapers that I got off eBay." He holds out one pot for me to observe. When I lean over the plant to sniff, my nose twitches and my eyes burn. "Don't want to get too close, dog boy. That there is the most potent pepper on the planet." He puts the pot back down on the table. "Like I said, Guy can't get enough of this stuff. But I know it's not for everybody, so I'll cook your grub separate."

"Thank you." I step from behind the plastic into the cool studio.

"Got any preferences?"

"Meat."

"Steak, lamb, chicken?"

I shrug because properly prepared they are equally appealing. "But if you don't mind, I prefer my meat quite rare."

"Me, I like my burgers and chops burnt to a crisp, but to each his own." Following Mason to the freight elevator, I sit by his feet awaiting the jaws to part to ride downstairs and explore the streets. "Where do you think you're going?"

"For a walk."

"Yo, Sniff, there ain't gonna be no walks. Guy says you're here to work, and so you're gonna work."

"Yes, of course, that will be my pleasure, and I am very grateful for the opportunity, but why can I not take my walk?"

"Listen, dog boy."

"My name is Piccolo."

"Right. Just remember what I told you about taking what's free and not asking any questions."

"Yes, of course."

"So, don't ask, okay? It's the way Guy wants it. And if it's the way Guy wants it, it's the way it's gonna be. So why don't you get started?" Mason steps into the elevator. "It'll make you feel better."

I know he is right, and so as the elevator descends to the ground floor, I walk back to the shelves of materials and take a roll of paper in my mouth which I carry into the open space of my studio and set down on the floor. I then reach for a stick of charcoal and with a kick of my front paw, unroll the paper before me. Crouching down on my haunches, I sketch out the shapes for my first series of art in America.

2 To Brooklyn

In the days that follow I work tirelessly, seldom taking off my goggles or work gloves as I concentrate on the blue arc that cuts through the lines I have drawn on the plates of stainless steel. My steady paw follows my sharp eye as I cut the organic and angular shapes that in the weeks that follow, I weld into sculpture—some titling, some upright, and one that appears to be collapsing.

With the magnificent tools that Mr. Guy Gizárd has provided and the freedom to work on a large-scale thanks to the overhead crane and hoist, my drawings spring from the pages of my sketchbook into three-dimensional form.

Days are no longer marked by light or no light, they are divided between work and fitful sleep in which I see only the lines I have made with a stick of soapstone on the metal meandering through my mind. Each day I wake, if not refreshed, resolved to create the next work. With my first pieces I have the luxury of space, being able to step back and see the evolving form. However, as weeks pass the lengths of stainless steel like weeds take over, and I work in a smaller and smaller area until I have laid the last bead of weld, and I have sculpted myself into a corner.

One day, though it is barely noon and far too early for my meal, I hear the clank and hum of the freight elevator. I brace myself to flee or fight.

"Yo, Sniff, it's only me. You look like you're ready to tackle a linebacker. Relax."

"Sorry, Mason, lack of sleep. My nerves are a little raw."

"No problem, I get it. Back in the day Guy'd get the same way, work day and night until he was like a crazy man."

"Does he not still work with the same fervor?"

"Not like he used to, but yo, he's still got plenty to do with the Biennial, you know, press releases, interviews, that sort of thing. Like I been bugging him every day this week to drive up to 57th to get fitted for the Fioravanti."

"I knew a Leo Fioravanti back in school."

"Not a Fioravanti, dog boy, the Fioravanti—the suit, huh? Like the finest in the world. Guy shells out more than a few grand every time he's got a show."

"With all these preparations, when does he have time to make sculpture?"

"Listen, at this stage of the game, he's not killing himself. And neither should you. Yeah, maybe it's a big thing for Guy, but for you it's just a show."

I walk to the other side of the studio feeling I am about to attack. It isn't Mason's fault that he cannot see that it is not only a show, it is the biggest chance of my life. With some exposure and sales, I'll be able to launch a full search for my papa and send home money to my mother who I know without me is having great difficulty pulling the cart to the Piazza to sell her watercolors.

Mason starts to take pictures of my work from every possible angle. "Guy wants to see what you've been up to. And so does Gloria. She's been bugging Guy for images to send out with the press release."

"Press release?"

"You know, PR to send around to critics. Art in America, Art Forum, Martin Kibbleman at the Times."

"Who is this Kibbleman?"

"You never heard of Martin Kibbleman? He's a big-time critic, mostly covers architecture, but for Guy he'll come out and cover a show."

"Of my work?"

"Yeah, well, of this work."

At this moment, I know I need to stretch my legs and run across an open piazza to calm my nerves.

I sit by the elevator, scratching at the door. "Mason, I must go out."

"No way, dog boy. You know the rules of the game. Water, grub and the best equipped studio in Williamsburg, but no going out."

If being assertive will not work, I decide to beg. "Please, Mason, I can't bear to pee into that water bowl, it's humiliating."

"What's humiliating is that I have to come behind you to flush."

"The flushing, it scares me," I say quite honestly as I take the end of a leash that hangs from a nail in my mouth. Desperate now, I whimper, indicating that I will even submit to being walked on the end of it.

"Go take a breather on the fire escape, but no going out on the street. Guy would have a fit."

I drop the handle of the leash from my mouth.

"Maybe he is your master, but he is not mine."

"Oh, really. You don't say. How are you any different than me? Other than you can't leave the stinking fourth floor—and me, on the other hand, I can come and go as I please."

"And always like a shackled man return."

Infuriated, Mason lunges at me grabbing my throat in his two thick hands while I thrash my head from side to side desperate to bite off his thumb. Only dimly am I aware of the sound of the descending elevator which returns and when the doors slowly part, Guy Gizárd emerges.

"Hey, hey, break it up you two," he yells, taking the leather leash from the wall and beating us both across our backs. But the sharp lashes only urge me to fight on until Guy runs to the room of pepper plants to grab the spray bottle, grasping and releasing the handle until the water that spits out from the nozzle brings me back to my senses.

Ashamed, I place my tail between my legs and retreat to my blanket in the far corner of the studio.

"What the hell, Mason! You're supposed to be taking care of this dog, not strangling it to death."

"Guy, he came at me. I was defending myself."

"Oh, yeah? It didn't look that way with your fat fingers around his throat."

"That dog is crazy."

"That dog is worth more than your life," says Gizárd, using a phrase I recall from that night on the ship when I jumped on his coat. Gizárd turns to me. "What's this all about anyway?"

Rising from the floor, I grasp the lock on the metal cage that secures the window. "It's about these bars. I need to go out."

At that moment, the musky smell of a female in heat rises from the street, even overpowering the aroma of the mortadella sausage sandwich I can smell coming from the wide pocket of Gizárd's leather coat.

"Listen, Piccolo, this is New York, and there's some things I want to keep out, and some I want to keep in."

"But I must be allowed to go out. I did not come to America to be your prisoner."

"Okay, now I get it. Now that you have a studio, my studio, full of the dog droppings you call art, you think you're going to call the shots."

At this moment I am torn between the desire to rip out the man's throat or grovel at his heels.

"You came to New York to make sculpture. And I made it happen. I pay the bills, and don't you forget that."

I remember what Guy Gizárd told me that first night on the ship. That in this city if you had no money, you were nobody. Nothing. And now I understand the stinging truth of those words because if I had money to board the ship back home to my life in Venice, I would leave this studio with my dignity intact.

"Now go lay down," shouts Gizárd. And to my shame, dear reader, I do.

But I cannot sleep. Throughout the night I stare into the forest of shadows cast by the columns in the light from the street. I now know that the strength or weakness of my reputation depends not on the work itself, but on the opinions of strangers. But who are these art critics? What does this man Kibbleman know of me, of my life or the generations of Fortunatos who have preceded me, whose dogged toil will contribute to my success or failure in America?

I sigh and put my muzzle on my paws, feeling no satisfaction from my great output of energy to complete this body of work. Instead I feel empty, worthless, and yes perhaps Guy Gizárd is right, and my sculptures, so meaningful in the making, are only dog droppings.

In a daze of self-loathing, I rise and stride into the storage room. I stare at the razor-sharp edges of my carving tools that have been useless on the workbench since the day I arrived. I recall Mason's message from Guy Gizárd: steel and only steel. I shake myself from head to tail as if I have fallen off a pier and swum back to shore where with my paws on solid ground, I feel revived.

I, Piccolo Fortunato, have been forbidden by a man to work in my own way, with my own paws on whatever material nature has provided me?

No. I will work in the way that pleases me, and at that moment I feel the urge to carve.

By the same twists of nature that have brought me to Brooklyn, so too has this cherry tree been cut down, hauled and hoisted into the window of this Morgan Avenue studio. I bow my head in gratitude and set to work.

Reaching for the Husqvarna on the shelf, I attack the wood with the short, sharp teeth of its roaring blade, losing all sense of self in that shower of splinters and chips, cutting, gouging, roughing out a form that demands to be freed from the wood. Cleansed by the sweet scent of that cherry wood, overwhelmed with the joy of free and unfettered creation, I allow my paws to move faster than my mind until I let the chainsaw fall to my side, and in the sudden silence, I step back to view the first stage of a work of art.

I stand humbled and elated as Mason enters.

"Here's your grub from last night. Guy told me to wait till you cooled off." He sets down the mix of kibble with fresh roasted chicken peeled from the bone. "Listen, I'm sorry about yesterday. We both got a little hot under the collar."

But I am so transfixed by the sculpture before me that his words are distant and confused, like the sound of a language I have never learned. And even though the pungent smell of the poultry draws my attention, I stand still.

"Are you listening to me?" But turning his eyes toward that which holds my attention, he too becomes silent. Finally, he murmurs. "Ah, *ma che bella*."

I nod my thanks to Mason whose words at that moment have far more weight than any New York Times art critic.

"This time, Piccolo, you have outdone yourself."

"Thanks, Mason," I say, my tail low and wagging.

"Really, I've seen a lot a stuff—studios, galleries, museums, you name it. But this, this one has something, something else. Something you want to reach out and touch but can't. You know what I mean?"

"Yes, I do. That is the same way I feel about my father. He has been gone from me for so long, and yet I feel he is so close that I can reach out and touch him, but I can't."

"Yo, there's more truth in that than you realize, dog boy. But I definitely can relate."

"Why, did you also lose your father at a young age?"

"More like he lost me. On purpose. He ditched me and my mom when I was like two, and then she ditched me when I was like seven."

"Ditches are low and lonely places."

"You telling me? I went from one uncle's basement to a cousin's couch until I got myself into a little trouble and got sent upstate for a couple years."

Lightly he taps the bowl with his white leather shoe in my direction. "Go ahead, *mangia*."

The word triggers my hunger, and I devour the pebbles of dog food moistened by the natural juices of the still hot chicken, continuing to glance up to let Mason know I am still listening.

"Yeah, well, old story, right? Anyway, that summer when I got back to the neighborhood, that's when Guy showed up on the block and pretty much took me under his wing."

I lick the drippings from the bottom of my bowl. "He is a generous man."

"Yes and no. But it's been a roof over my head, and like I said, I'd do anything for Guy."

I follow Mason to the far end of the loft where in the small kitchen he sets down two brown bags on the counter. From them arise a complex blend of aromas: raw meat, goat cheese, scallions and a mixture of pungent smells that I begin to untangle as I sniff the air. "What are those?"

Mason lines up several small sacks on the counter. "You got your basic cumin, coriander, turmeric, you know, spices for the masala, which tonight at Guy's request is gonna have a special kick."

"Mr. Gizárd is coming here?"

"Yeah, with Gloria Gallstone."

"Here tonight? I don't think that I am ready."

"It's not about when you think you're ready, dog boy, it's up to Guy. He liked what he saw yesterday, and he says it's time."

"But I have just made this work, and already it is going to be taken to the gallery?"

"Yeah, well, a New York minute, right? Just go lay down and relax until they get here."

"I can't relax," I say pacing the hardwood floor.

From the bag marked Trader Joe's, Mason takes a glass bottle filled with a yellow beverage. When he pops off the cap that bounces off the counter, it fizzles, bubbling up and onto the grey marble. "Taste it, see if you like it."

I lick the counter and snap my tongue off the roof of my mouth, considering the taste. "Not bad."

He pours the foaming liquid into my bowl. "Corona. It'll calm you down."

Thirsty from my long day's work, I lap up the drink he calls Corona. It makes me sneeze several times, but I like it so much I scratch the empty bowl for him to pour in the rest of the bottle.

"Now drink it and settle down, I got work to do. They'll be here by eight—but you know, a really good vindaloo ought'a be made like two days in advance."

Mason now seems to be talking to himself as he clicks a flame under the heavy skillet, pours in olive oil and then peels three onions.

"It takes at least a day for the meat to sop up all the flavor—but no not Guy, he just springs it on me this morning like it's no big deal. So I say, okay, how about I get some lamb, grape leaves, feta and I do Greek? But he says no, he wants vindaloo."

Now Mason speaks to the gleaming blade of his chef's knife as his hand a blur, he thinly slices the onions that he tosses into the hot oil. He then slits two jalapeños, cutting them into thin strips that he scrapes from the cutting board into the pan.

"So, what am I gonna do? Guy says, vindaloo, it's vindaloo."

Mason whacks the knife with the side of his fist to split open the garlic that he minces and scrapes into the oil with a sizzle that reminds me of home.

I lean on the counter to watch with interest as he unwraps the brown paper, releasing the smell of the fresh-cut chunks of slightly marbleized meat. He tosses me the biggest one which I gratefully catch mid-air while from his other massive hand, he drops fistfuls of beef onto the skillet to sear.

Then, into a small glass bowl he grates ginger, adding spices and sugar before splashing in the vinegar. As he whisks the mixture, his golden chains lightly jangle around his fat wrist.

The wet masala hits the pan. It sizzles wildly, bubbling up in a fury until Mason turns the flame down low. He then slips behind the plastic sheet where the hot lamps warm the earthen pots, and he emerges with two slightly bent chili peppers and a third that looks like a paper lantern of an even darker, more ominous shade.

"We got two serranoes and a reaper. A dash of my Mason's special blend, and this'll be the vindaloo to end all vindaloos."

As he slits them open, I blink my eyes and sneeze.

"Mama always scoops out the seeds."

"Well, this is not your mamma's pepper."

Mason seems unaffected as he slices, but my nostrils quiver and burn. "This stuff ain't for virgins, dog boy. You better go lay down. But don't worry, for you tonight's gonna be some good eats."

"I did like the kibble and chicken, Mason, but maybe next time you can add a little olive oil and basil?"

"It's gonna be something way better than chicken. Guy brought you home a special treat."

"Really?" I am taken aback that on top of all his generosity, Mr. Gizárd is bringing me a special treat.

I cannot help but ask. "Mason, what is it?"

"Well, I'm not supposed to tell you. But some mega-collector from Taiwan took him to Luger's for lunch, and he's got like a pound of porterhouse that he brought back for you. You know, a doggie bag."

I have never heard the word doggie, which I do find demeaning, but given the way Mason raises his brow when he says porterhouse, I am far more interested in what that might be.

"What exactly is this porterhouse?"

"It's the best cut—you got your T-bone with your tenderloin and your strip steak side by side." The Corona has made my head feel light, and I tilt it trying to decipher his meaning.

"Steak, dog boy, steak. He's bringing home a doggie bag with leftover steak."

"Leftover? Who does not finish a steak?"

"Guy. When like every other day some collector, curator, museum big shot takes him out for lunch. Yeah, he's gotta schmooze, but he don't like to eat in the afternoon, so for him it's mostly liquid lunch. Cocktails, whisky. He pretty much saves his appetite for home. At least back in the day, he always did."

"Well, it is very nice of him to bring me this special treat. I will go lie down and think of it with anticipation."

"You do that, Sniff. I got plenty to do."

Crossing to my blanket in the far corner of the loft, I curl up beneath the open window and inhale deeply the smell of cement after an early summer rain mingling with the yeasty aroma of dough rising and the light sharp scent of tomato sauce from the pizzeria down the street.

Exhausted from not having slept in two days, my mind drifts off on a cloud of Corona. All the stress in my muscles dissolves as my paws move in the air and I dream of chasing pigeons across the Piazza until I am startled by a clang, and then the birds fly off and the flutter of their thousand wings becomes the hum of the rising freight elevator.

I listen to the muffled words of Guy Gizárd overlapping with a high pitched and startling voice. I cannot make out the conversation until the doors open, and I hear the click-clacking of a woman's shoes on the hardwood floors.

"Oh, Guy, this work is magnificent."

"Yeah, it's good, but it ain't that good." I hear a lighter open, snap and shut as a pungent, weedy smell intermingles with the waves of Mason's vindaloo that fills the studio.

As the evening light streams through the window, Gloria Gallstone makes her way through the maze of shadows and steel. From my blanket I pretend to sleep, but from beneath my barely open lids, I observe her movements as she gravitates toward the serpentine form of the piece I call *Sniff*. She runs her hand lightly over the surfaces and looks closely at the welds.

"Mason!" Gizárd shouts from his perch on the sill.

Obediently Mason emerges from the kitchen. "Yeah, Guy?"

"What time is that kid supposed to show up?"

"Plane gets in at nine, want me to go pick him up?"

"No. Let him find his own way, I'm tired of coddling these newbies."

The sound of the heels grows sharper as the woman crosses the studio toward me. "And this must be the Italian greyhound I've heard so much about."

Before I can fully rise, she is standing over my blanket and patting my head. Not knowing the proper thing to do when meeting a powerful gallery owner, I also stand and lick her hand.

"So, Guy tells me you're from Venice."

"Yes, I am."

"I just love Venice. I have a beautiful place overlooking the Grand Canal, not far from the Gritti. Granted, it's not on a ground floor above a flooded basement, but I do call it home when I'm there."

My brow furrows, betraying my confusion. On one hand, she seems so gracious and charming, yet I wonder if Guy has told her of my mother's limited means and how she was forced to move us into a damp and ill-lit ground floor room. And with that information has Gloria Gallstone just insulted me?

By the way she continues to laugh as her host hands her the loosely rolled cigar, I decide that she has. And that here is a human, despite the Prada bag and Gucci shoes—all three of which I feel a strong desire to chew—of a rather low nature.

"Now, now, puppy, I am just joking." Although she is scratching behind my ear in a way I find unpleasant, I contain myself and gently nudge my nose against her knee which by the way she chuckles, she seems to like. Although younger in human years than my mother, she lacks my mother's natural elegance and grace.

"So, you made all of this in what—nine, ten weeks?"

"Quite honestly, when I work, I lose all sense of time."

"Hmm, to lose one's sense of time, that's rather transcendent." She ponders, unclasping the Prada bag that I so want to bite. She takes out the flat device that I have often seen both locals and tourists in Venice carry tilted in their hands, barely looking up to see the interplay of light on the architecture of the Piazza. As they do, she taps rapidly with her thumbs on the screen.

"Yes, transcendent, I do like that word. It's been a long time since I had reason to use it, wouldn't you agree, Guy?"

"Yeah, well, I always made art with my eye on the clock."

"Yes, and on somebody else's bank account." Gloria Gladstone emits another thin laugh.

"True. I'm gonna check on dinner, you keep schmoozing." Crossing to the kitchen, he takes his silver flask from his pocket and tips it back.

"While Guy keeps boozing," she whispers, leaning toward my ear in an oddly conspiratorial way. She sticks out her hand on which I place my paw. "We haven't been properly introduced, have we? I'm Gloria, Gloria Gallstone, and I believe your name is Niccolo?"

"Piccolo, Piccolo Fortunato."

"A grand name for a young dog with grand prospects."

I am taken aback by the praise and tilt my head to try to determine the level of this gaunt woman's sincerity.

"Really," she says, seeming to sense my suspicion. "I loved the work the minute I walked in. Tell me about it."

"The pieces are loosely based on a number of sketches I had shown to Mr. Gizárd. And then when I came to the studio, I took a stick of soapstone and started to sketch them out on plates of stainless…"

"No, no, no. Tell me what you were thinking when you were making these pieces."

"When I work, I do not think."

"Oh excellent, doesn't think." Gallstone continues to tap on her device. "Let's call it an intuitive approach." Then she glances down at me again. "Well, if your work is not about a thought process, what is it about?"

"Smell."

"Excuse me? I don't understand."

"Tell me, what do you smell?"

"You—want me—to tell you what I smell?" she asks with the ends of her mouth curling slightly.

"Yes." I sniff the air to demonstrate.

"Okay, I'll play along. For a minute. Garlic, some sort of curry?"

"I also smell each pungent wave of cumin, coriander and turmeric intertwining in the air, and the moist earth— a complex smell of soil, earthworms, fungi and bacteria—from which the garlic was plucked."

"Go on."

I inhale more deeply. "I smell the wet green leaves that were pushed aside to pick a flower with its seeds, the smell of a latex glove on the hand that operated the grinding machine and the hundred hands that filled the sacks, packed the trucks and shipped those many spices to a place called Trader Joe's to be purchased by Mason, who has his own distinct scent, to simmer in that pot, creating the smells that you call some sort of curry."

"That's a rather whimsical analysis."

"Not an analysis, just observation—through smell of the connectedness of all things." Gallstone now sniffs the air herself to better discern my meaning.

"And what do you smell in the sourness of the vinegar?"

I close my eyes and expand my nostrils. "That is no mere vinegar, but rather the ambrosia of Modena where the white *Trebbiano di Castelvetro* grapes are pressed. And in it I can sniff every scent of my homeland."

"That's a lot of crap," says Mr. Gizárd from the far end of the studio.

"Guy, you're jaded. Ignore him, tell me more. What were you smelling when you made this?" She runs her finger along the welded seam of a horizontal piece I call *Sill*.

"I remember that morning well when on the windowsill I detected the odor of fresh pigeon droppings and glancing over I saw a squirrel that looked back at me with startled eyes as it cracked open an acorn between its teeth. So, there is an element of sound and fear in this piece as well."

With a bottle of wine in his hand, Mr. Gizárd crosses to the table over which Mason has spread a white cloth and set with two plates, but no bowl. As he twists the corkscrew, he shakes his head with disgust.

"Hey, Mason, gimme a double of whatever the dog's been drinking."

"Oh, be quiet, Guy," says Gallstone who returns her attention to me. "I believe Guy told me you're what? Three years old?"

"Yes, I am three."

"You seem quite knowledgeable for one so young."

"Each dog day is equivalent to your week, each month more than half a year. So even in the time since I arrived here in your city, I have much matured."

Brazenly the woman pats my upper and lower trapezius muscles which from my hard weeks of labor in the studio sleekly bulge.

"Yes, I see you have." She squeezes my loin in a way that makes my hind leg twitch. As I scratch, she then moves toward another sculpture, a squat, angular piece that appears to be caving in on itself. "And what were you thinking, I mean smelling, when you made this one?"

"You know, I've heard a lot of bull crap before, but give me a break." The cork slides against glass of the bottle with a sleek squeak and a pop. "This is more than I can take sober."

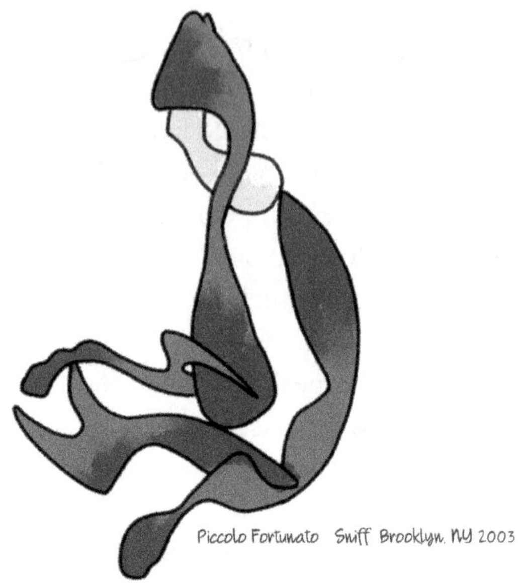

Again, the woman bends secretively toward my ear. "And when was Guy ever that?"

Guy pours and drains a glass of wine in two swift parts of the same motion. "Just gimme a chance to catch up."

Mason sets two large steaming bowls on the table. "Hey, Guy, must've been the Corona. He lapped that beer right up."

"Well, crack him open another, and maybe he'll go back to sleep," says Gizárd with a derisive laugh.

Insulted, I walk away.

"No, ignore them, do tell me more."

Preferring not to be ridiculed, I shake my head and make my way toward my blanket.

"No, don't listen to them. I am intrigued. What do you call this one?"

"Doom."

"And what smell do you associate with Doom?"

"Gasóleo."

"Diesel fuel? Why?"

"It is the smell of your extinction." I circle the blanket and fluff it with my teeth before tucking my legs under me and lying down with my muzzle pointed toward the wall.

"Brilliant," mutters Gallstone who continues tapping on her device. "How about this, Guy? An intuitive approach to the complexity, no, the multivalence of smell. Yes, an intuitive approach to the multivalence of smell from a canine perspective."

"You're not going to write that crap, are you?"

"I most certainly am. In fact, it's just what I need for this press release I'm shooting off to Martin."

"So, you're saying I'm a dog."

"No, Guy, that this new work embodies an intuitive approach to the multivalence of smell from a canine perspective. There sent. I'm not saying you are a dog, I'm saying you smell like a dog."

"Oh, that's just great."

"That you can identify with the senses of a dog, your own visceral sensibility. Is that better?"

"Listen, Gloria, minimal has worked for twenty years."

"Try thirty, Guy, and yes it did, but sales are way down and quite frankly you're teetering on the edge of irrelevance."

"Me, Guy Gizárd, irrelevant? Never."

"These days what hasn't been done to death? And this whole notion of olfaction in art is so new, so compelling. The collectors will eat it up, or should I say sniff. Trust me, Guy, you needed a concept and this is it. Your show will sell out."

I feel my ears rise and my brow furrow. "His show?"

"Why of course," says Gallstone who sits down, crossing her weak legs and tossing her hand over the back of the chair as she turns to face me. "After all, Niccolo, you are just an intern."

There is a pause in the room when only the splash of wine being poured by Mason into her glass can be heard. Then Gallstone turns her attention to the table.

"Guy, really? Wine with curry?"

"Yeah, why not?" His words are muffled by the food in his

mouth. "Oh, that's hot, that's good."

She reaches for the bottle and reads the label as Mason spoons the food onto her plate.

"The guy in the store said it's a good match."

"Stormhoek Pinotage, South African, interesting." She sets down the bottle before taking a forkful of the glistening meat to her mouth. Her eyes pop slightly as she raises the napkin from her lap to her lips. "Oh, Guy," she croons as Mason retreats toward the kitchen. "This vindaloo is to die for!"

The sound of a horse fly buzzing about my ear drowns out their conversation. Lying on the floor, staring at the sheetrock, I have a vision. It is late one summer evening heading home with Mama from the market, crossing the Ponte di Rialto when a storm breaks out over the lagoon and a crack of lightning splits the sky and all of Venice is for one moment revealed.

So do I at this moment see my journey in one panoramic view— from the moment I first saw Guy Gizárd vomiting over the rail of the *Preziosa* to when she docked in New York Harbor, and I came to this Williamsburg studio that all along has been no more than my prison—I have been duped.

At times nature is cruel, and at times merciful. Overcome with a heavy sleep from my weeks of creative labor, I become no more than a breathing mass of bones and fur.

3 And Back

Between my eyes I feel three hard scratches and forcing my lids open with much effort, I see the Gucci shoes and my jaws snap. Gloria Gallstone pulls away her white tipped fingers, and if she had not done so quickly, I would have bitten her hand.

"Oh my, now that's a change of attitude." She turns and strides toward the elevator. "Great, dinner, Guy. Handle that." And as the doors close, she descends. Although my back is to him, I can feel my fur rise at the man's approach.

"I know. Gloria comes off like a first-class bitch."

In no mood for bad jokes, I snarl.

"Listen, kid, it's just the business. She's really a sweetheart. But I get it. It's a shocker when you come out into the world. You're young, you're fresh, you're half-pup, half-man, but there's nothing out here that your mama could've prepared you for."

I bare my teeth at the mention of my mother.

"It's just the way the art world works. Let me explain something to you." He sets his drink down on the sill and eases himself onto the floor beside me. "You know what a pyramid is, right? It's like that. People like Gloria are toward the top, and she makes money representing a big name like me who gets dog boys like you to make the work."

"Then it is not your work."

"There you're right, and you're wrong. Yeah, it's not my work, my sweat, but it is my work, my property. Number one, because I am the artist. I'm not supposed to sweat, I am the one with the ideas."

"That's a lie. All these forms are from my mind."

"Your forms were an afterthought, kid. The first thought was mine that night on the deck. It was my idea to bring you here, to set you up to make this work. For me. Which brings us back to reason number two. I paid for it. I pay for this space, I pay for your food, I pay for Mason's cheap cologne, and I pay him to take care of you. See these pieces, all these pieces, no matter how many fancy words you attach to them, the prime idea, the numero uno, to bring you here to make them, was mine. And that's what makes me the artist, and you the flunky."

I stare directly into Gizárd's blood shot eyes. My ears flick back and with my lips are drawn over my teeth, and I emit a long, low growl.

"Oh, yeah, you're threatening me? You're not the first, kid, and you won't be the last. But you're all the same. I house you, feed you, keep you off the street, and then like all the rest of them when the time comes to turn over what's mine, you turn on me. When in fact if you were as smart as pretend to be, you'd follow my lead. Put some time in at Studio Gizárd, pay your dues, and then one day you've got your own studio, and some hungry young studs working for you, *capiche*?"

"No, I do not understand how an artist preys on other artists. Dogs do not eat the flesh of other dogs."

"Yeah, but you got no trouble chewing the meat off a chicken leg and then crunching down on the bone. Interns are my chickens— and stick with me, kid, and they can be yours. You can be the top dog. Just swallow a little of that Fortunato pride. What do you say?"

Guy Gizárd kneels beside me, reeking of wine and whisky, and the smell of the meat he has consumed as it oozes from his oily skin has no appeal. I stand up, leaving Guy Gizárd on all fours. I walk to the shelf and place my chisels and awls back into my leather tool roll.

"Okay, okay, I get it. All for you, nothing for me."

He grabs hold of the sill to pull himself up, then follows me to the place on the wall where from a nail my duffel bag hangs, sagging with the weight of my torch. I unpin my sketches from the wall, placing them between the pages of my portfolio.

"But listen, kid, I want you to remember this. Guy Gizárd is not the greedy bastard some people make him out to be. What I got, I share."

I am about to place my carving tools in the canvas bag when from the kitchen he brings out a package that he unwraps and holds in his open hands to display the pound of steak that stands out boldly against the silver paper. I have never seen meat like it before—moist and succulent, yet its edges are seared black. The smell is overwhelming.

"There you go. I knew I could get a wag out of you." He raises it just high enough that I cannot reach it, but I am overpowered by the smell. My nostrils quiver as I sniff the air—a smell somewhere between flesh still warm on the bones of a fresh kill, and the charred edge of a wedge of meat pulled out of a fire on a stick and tossed to my ancestor, ravenous after the hunt.

I feel angry at myself for showing desire, but my tail continues to wag and drool hangs from my mouth. Weeks of physical exertion have depleted me, and the meat calls to me in an ancient way. Eat now and eat fast because you might not eat again.

When the man sets the meat on the floor, I fall upon it with a gusto I have never known, tearing the beef from the bone that I brace against the floor with one paw. And that is where I feel the burn first like I have stepped on fire. But unable to stop my teeth from grinding, I am swallowing the flame that lights my throat like a match and incinerates my stomach.

Gizárd falls back laughing as the elevator opens, and Mason enters with a travel-worn Doberman on the same short chain with which I had been taken from the ship.

"Guy, what did you do to him?"

"The only way to reason with a dog is through his stomach."

Mason picks up the T-bone and sniffs the remaining meat. "You doused it, Guy. You didn't have to do that."

"Oh, now you're gonna start with me? Gimme that leash and get that one the hell out of here."

I roll on the floor with my two paws clawing uselessly at my muzzle. I choke and vomit and then choke some more.

"Put him in the cellar. And you, newbie, clean up that mess." He is pointing to the pile of puke and meat on the floor. Mason hands the Doberman's leash to Guy, and while grabbing hold of my collar, pulls me into the elevator. As we descend, I see through the open mesh of the gate the Doberman become its legs, and its legs become its paws, and then it becomes a mouth at Gizárd's feet that devours the mess of meat and kibble.

I want to bark, I want to bite, but my mouth is aflame, and the searing pain spills out of my watery eyes. The elevator stops with a jolt and through the gate a blast of cold, damp air gives no relief.

"Why'd you have to go and piss Guy off?" Mason releases my collar and pushes me into the darkness that without my sense of smell, is truly dark and full of unseen danger.

I hear the gate close behind me and the clank and hum of the ascending elevator, a hum that blends with a low growl. Close, closer, and then it is upon me.

The fury of its spit splatters me as the shadow dog hurls its body at my chest and goes directly for my throat. Though it is diminutive, this dog is lean and vicious.

On the ground, the pain inside my organs rising to greet the pain of my pierced skin, I shake myself from my confusion and lunge, forcing off the attacker. I hear the thud of its body against a wall that it uses to catapult itself onto my back where it grips and rips my ear.

I flip it off me, then sensing its age and feeling the power of my youth, I set my jaws on its throat and prepare to end this battle. Until I hear the raspy tone of a voice that tolls like la Marangona. "Son, son, my son."

I release my fangs from the skin that has nearly split beneath the pressure of my bite. Without my eyes or sense of smell, I have to rely on a deeper sense that indeed this is my father. The fluid draining from my eyes, my nostrils and my mouth flows more heavily upon him as with his rough tongue he licks my muzzle.

"Piccolo."

"Papa." I bark as we spring up and leap around like young pups, bouncing, weaving, crouching, bobbing.

"How can this be?" And as I bow my head, he licks my wounded ear. The flames still flicker throughout my organs, but the balm of my father's tongue soothes every pain.

And then as in the darkness of the cinema, my mind projects an image before me of the marble sculpture by the Roman artist that we had long ago admired at the Vatican—of two greyhounds side-by-side, one licking the other's ear. Only now instead of being viewers, we have become that work of art.

"Oh, Papa." I collapse beside him like a puppy, all the fight, all the struggle, all the anger gone. I lie beside him with my wounded ear on his chest, listening to the beat that so deeply calms me.

"But how is it that you come to be here in this darkness? Or is this just an image that I've conjured in my mind to convince myself to live through another faceless night."

"It is I, Piccolo. And I was brought here from the ship by the man who lied."

"Yes, I met the same man, and despite my age and the wisdom I should have possessed, I too believed him which is how I came to be in this odorless hell."

"Papa, are you blind?"

"I can smell nothing. It began when I refused to make more work for him to place in their mausoleums."

"Museums." I correct him, saddened that his senses have become so dim that he has lost sight of the meaning of the word.

"No, son, mausoleums, spaces to inter bodies of dead work, art that no one can touch and touches no one. I wanted no part of it."

Alert I listen as when I was a pup to my father's words, always meaty with new meaning, heavy with a bone on which to later gnaw.

"But Gizárd forced me—starving me for weeks on end, and then putting steak before me, laced with the devil sauce."

"Yes, Papa, he did the same to me tonight."

"And over time, if the work did not sell, he increased the fire—but if a curator, collector, a critic called, and there was a sale, review, a show? Then he would reduce the fiery sauce. But over time as baneful as the chili was to my sense of smell, I craved it as only the physical pain could distract me from the pain I felt in my heart. And I waited with my tail between my legs for Mason to bring me my next taste of the Carolina Reaper."

"Oh, Papa, he will pay."

"Not by any act of ours, but yes, according to the laws of nature which exceed the laws of men, Guy Gizárd will pay."

The familiar hum of the elevator now sounds an alarm of an enemy's approach, and I feel my hackles rise. Strengthened by our bond, we stand in the dark together with our legs bent and our bodies taut and ready to lunge.

"Hey, dog boy, I see you found your dog dad."

Together our snarls warn that we will attack. "Whoa, dogs, whoa. I'm not here to hurt you, that's Guy's thing, not mine."

Our growls curl and spring into a volley of barks.

"Easy there, boys, easy." Mason moves slowly, opening the gate only wide enough to set down a bowl on the ground. "There you go, that'll help put out the burn."

Then the box ascends to the first floor where Mason switches on a light that seeps through the shaft. Whatever Mason has left in the ceramic bowl radiates coolness. My father bends his head over the white mounds and takes a lick.

"Perhaps that man does have a heart."

"Why, what is it, Papa?"

"Gelato."

I sniff the cool halo above the bowl and welcome it like the snow that sometimes falls lightly over Venice—as remarkable in its appearance as the sweet taste of the gelato that soothes my tongue. I lap it up, and the chill flows down my throat and fills my stomach. In a moment it is gone, as briefly beautiful as the white flakes on the paving stones of the Piazza.

Stepping back from the empty bowl, I realize what I have done. "I'm sorry, Papa. I have eaten it all."

"No, Piccolo, you gave me the lion's share just watching you."

Papa stands half my height and must stretch his neck to nuzzle my jowls as I lick the top of his head.

"Your ear is bleeding. Lie down."

Obediently I settle down beside him on the ground, and throughout the night his rough tongue nurses my wound. Days maybe weeks go by, marked only by Mason's appearance to refill my father's bucket with fresh water from a hose that runs down the elevator shaft. At those times he tosses a fistful of kibble and a fistful of meat into the silver bowl—from which I step back to let my father eat first.

He tells me the story of his passage to this city, a tale almost identical to my own, except for the years spent in this cellar that nearly drove him mad.

"I paced, hours upon hours, days upon days. My job was to chase down the rats, rough them up so they'd stay away. One time I got bitten and so sick, I prayed for death to take me, but it did not come, and I knew that nature had intended me to live. But never in a million dog years, did I in my tortured mind imagine you would be beside me here—a joy and a grief."

"Our grief is over, Papa," I whisper as my ears tilt back and my hackles rise in anticipation. "I sense the time to escape is near."

And indeed, it is so near that we both turn our heads to follow the movement of light on the brick wall that now illuminates our cell.

"Relax, relax, it's only me. I took the back stairs." We blink into the light and see Mason approach. "I didn't want to run into Guy on the way down." He sets down the duffel bag heavy with my tools and points past the brick wall. "That's the Morgan Avenue side. There's a steel door that's been padlocked for like thirty years. Don't know how it got past the inspectors without a violation, but whatever—you'll need this."

He takes out the torch I had brought with me from Italy, and I lick his hand, grateful for the return of my tool. "Thank you, Mason, but what good is a torch without tanks?"

Mason snaps his fingers, a sign for us to follow. Walking behind him, we come to a wall over which he sweeps the orb of light that for a moment settles on a black and dented form in the corner.

The object seems to call to me. I lift and pass the battered hat to my father who stares at it, nodding in recognition. "My old friend," he says brushing off the cobwebs from his pork pie hat. With its flat crown and broad rim balanced perfectly between his ears, I remember the look of my papa from better times.

"Nice." Mason shines the light fully on my father whose silhouette stands out like a painting on the wall of this cave.

We continue down the dark corridor following the beam of light that searches the wall. "Oh, *mannaggia*, where's the friggin' door?" Then settling on an exit sign, the light moves downward to reveal the perpendicular seams of a doorway. "Hold this."

Mason hands me the flashlight while with his shoulder he rams the metal door. It takes three hard hits, but finally it gives way into another chamber where light seeps in around the edges of the newspapers that cover the narrow windows, level with the street.

"I haven't been down here since Guy had me seal it off." Mason walks over to where two sawhorses stand beneath a plate of steel that has over time been coated with a patina of grime and mouse droppings.

My father runs his paw over the steel. "Abandoned," he murmurs, examining the curf that had been cut halfway across the surface of the steel and then abruptly ended.

"Back in the day Guy rented this space for like a buck and a half a month. He slept over there on a cot and worked over here. In the summer he used to open that cellar door and let us kids come down and watch. But then Guy got big, Gizzard became Gizárd, and that was that. The end of an era." He flashes the light to a corner where chained to a tool cart stands a pair of tanks, one tall and green flanked by a shorter black one. "There you go, you got your basic oxy and acetylene. Guess you still remember what to do with those, huh, Pops?" Mason takes a pair of goggles from his pocket and tosses them to my father.

"Does a baker forget how to knead? But this is not my job." My father tosses the goggles to me. "This is a job for Piccolo."

With my tail wagging, I dig through my bag for my leather gloves and sparker that I place on the plate of steel beside my torch.

"Well, there's your way out." He points to where a heavy padlock hangs over a six-inch-wide hasp that is hinged to the wall. "Get through that and it'll take you right out onto the street where I got the jeep parked."

"But why, Mason, why now?"

"Listen, Pops, just because it didn't work out for me and my old man, don't mean you two can't have a better ending. Anyways, tonight is the night."

I attach the hoses and adjust the valves, keeping an eye on the gauges. "What night?"

"The opening, Sniff—your pieces at the Gallstone Gallery. The dad dog'll be proud."

My tail sags. "Why? To see my work exhibited under that man's name?"

"Who cares about a name, it's still your work."

"Yes, son, and I will view it with great excitement," Papa says wagging his tail.

Both males watch as holding my torch, I open the valve and strike my sparker, releasing the long yellow flame that feathers with a seam of soot rising from the edge. When I open the oxygen, the untethered flame draws inward, tamed into a stream of pale blue light—a shimmering cylinder that encircles the sharper, dark blue flame at the tip of my torch.

I reach for a stick of soapstone from the makeshift table and draw a line across the shackle of the lock on which I focus the tiny blue jets. When the steel burns with a fiery glow, I grip the lever to release the oxygen, then guide the tip slowly across the line until with a thud the padlock falls to the dirt floor.

"Good job, Sniff," says Mason. Setting down the torch, I reach for a piece of angle iron that I use to pry open the door. With the sounds from the street, the summer evening floods down the stairwell and decades of dust rise up. My father steps back into the shadows as I vault up the concrete steps.

Mason takes a tiny device from his pocket, points it in the direction of the street and clicks, a sound to which his car responds with a tweet. "Okay, boys, show time!" he says hurrying up after me. But my father doesn't follow.

"Papa, what's wrong?" I call down from the sidewalk to where my father has stepped back into the cellar, cowering. And for the first time in that light, I can see how the years alone have drained him, not only of his strength, but his belief in himself.

"It's been too long, Piccolo. You go, I am just a rat chaser, and I no longer have a place in the world."

"Papa, like me you are a Fortunato, and we share our place in the long line of Fortunatos, those that have passed and those who will follow. Come!" I run back to him and nudge him up the stairs to the street with my muzzle.

"Yo, dogs, let's ride!" Mason calls from the jeep where he leans across to open the door on the passenger side. With some difficulty my father climbs onto the cream-colored seat.

After I close the door and he is safely inside, a spring pops inside of me, and my legs take off at full throttle as my body stretches and soars. I turn the corner of the block and am running along the sidewalk when a motorcycle in the street revs and roars and challenges me. I race past the blur of sound when from above I hear applause and cheers that blend with the facades of buildings. With each stride my lungs heave back my thanks to nature for light and air and speed to round the corner of this Brooklyn block, sailing past the chain link fence of a vacant lot to return to the spot where I now meet my father's face, beaming with pride from the rolled down window.

"Well done, son."

I bow my head before leaping into the back seat while Mason turns the key in the ignition, pulls away from the curb and takes off for Manhattan.

"Sit back and enjoy the ride, boys, we're taking the scenic route—BQE to the Brooklyn Bridge and then straight up the West Side."

Driving along this elevated skyway that Mason calls the BQE, we are level with the rooftops where up ahead a flock of pigeons rises and arcs, flying in a circling formation. I look down at the streets that I recall from the first day Mason had driven me to Brooklyn. They are less strange to me now as I have taken in their smells from the open window of the studio. But now I know that I have earned my place on them—these are my streets, the smells are my smells, and as my tongue lolls from my mouth and my ears fly back in the wind, I feel the joy of a young dog about to make my mark on this City of York they call New.

"Hey, dad dog, you like jazz, right?" Mason turns on the radio and moves through a blur of voices and flashes of music. "88.3, best jazz station in the world. Me? I like a little salsa, bachata, but when Guy's in the car, it's WBGO all the way." The bright tones of a tenor sax fill the car and blow out the window with the end of summer breeze.

"*My Favorite Things.*" I yap in recognition of the album of the same name by the great John Coltrane that my father used to play each morning before he set to work in his studio. I recall the blue cover of the album and the oily sheen of the record on which he would place the needle of the stereo that had been his prized possession. I was with him when he found it on the Grand Canal, neatly bagged to be picked up by the hoist of the garbage barge. All this comes back to me as we listen, watching the city roll by.

"Yeah," says Mason driving with one arm out the window while my father's head sways. "It don't get better than this. Check out lady liberty, boys, she's looking hot tonight."

Indeed, the sight of the green lady fills my heart with joyful anticipation. We are on the bridge now, and I tilt my head to better view the crisscrossing cables and the walkway which move above us. I lean forward between the two front seats and nudge my father's head as he has been very quiet.

"Papa, are you okay?"

"At this moment I am better than okay, for this is the America that as a pup I dreamed of. And even in my prison, this is the America I knew still existed."

"I'm glad your dream came true, Pops. But listen," says Mason in a tone of voice I have never heard from him before. "I'm sorry, dog dad. It shouldn't have taken that long." And then looking intently at my father, he misses his exit. "Jeez, I don't want the East Side." Hitting the brakes, he throws the jeep into reverse. "Don't worry, I got this." He throws a kiss to the driver of the van who curses him loudly. "I'm taking you guys up the West Side to get a good look at the Hudson."

And indeed, it is a pleasant sight at this hour when a soft light roams over the faces of the people who stroll along the promenade. A swarm of cyclists races by, but as we overtake them, I turn my head and bark in admiration of their speed. I particularly enjoy the cool, moist breeze that blows off the river and makes my jowls flap.

"This is it, Sniff. You wanted Chelsea, you got Chelsea." Mason then takes the 23rd Street exit and drives down a street toward a yellow flag where he pulls up on the sidewalk and into a parking garage, moist and poorly lit, that makes me think of that ground floor room where Mama waits for us still.

I have not told Papa of our hardship in his absence. Although I am sure he knows, I felt he was too weak to remind him of that pain. But as we walk from the garage and down a tree-lined street where we both piss somewhat urgently, I decide it is time to tell him.

"You know Mama misses you."

"I know, my son. And I know how hard it's been for you both. But I also know that despite the softness of a greyhound's skin, we are strong animals, and that even in my absence she raised you to be a strong male."

The moisture from my tear ducts fills my nostrils, and I sneeze twice. When I glance up at Mason, I see that with the handkerchief from his breast pocket he is dabbing his own eyes.

"Males," says my father suddenly, and regaining the former strength and timbre of his voice, he tilts his muzzle skyward, and his lips resonate with a haunting series of ancestral sounds—ah-rooo, ah-rooo. And standing beside him as we wait for the traffic light to change, Mason and I lift our snouts and bay toward the rooftops of the town they call Chelsea.

"Mason, take us to a bàcaro where we can enjoy some polpette and a bowl of wine."

"Forget the cicchetti, Pops. I'm taking you two guys out for a full-blown Italian dinner, there's a seafood joint around the block. One of the partners is a friend of mine, well, of Guy's, so we'll get a table no problem."

I follow Mason, but taking a sniff of myself, I realize that I have been in the filthy cellar after weeks of non-stop work.

"Mason," I say pulling him by the sleeve toward the curb. "Do I smell okay to you?"

"Listen, Sniff, don't worry about it. You're an artist, you're old school. It's just your style. Besides, you're with me."

Remaining unconvinced by any of his loosely reasoned arguments, I step back from the stone façade of the restaurant and hesitate at the thick black door that he holds open.

"I'm telling you don't worry about it, this place is casual." Then leaning toward my ear he adds, "The guy I was telling you about, the chef? He's a fisherman, stinks like fish. Listen, if he comes by the table, don't tell him I told you so, okay?"

As my father has already passed through the entrance, I follow with my eyes lowered on the black and white marble tiles. But descending the plank stairs, I feel encouraged by the warmth of the voices within—waiting for, chatting over, finishing their food. Aroused by the smells that arise from the plates, I lift my head and feel my eyes widen at the sight of a beautiful woman who raises a forkful of charred *polipo* to her mouth. Enchanted I sit down beside her table and stare with equal intensity at both the plump morsel and her plump lips.

"*Bella donna,*" I say softly with a smile the way they do to draw pleasant attention. And when she smiles back with a bit of parsley on her gleaming tooth, I am about to engage her in a conversation about the preparation of baby octopus—to tell her how back home in Venice we lightly boil the succulent creatures, tossing our *folpeti* with virgin olive oil and lemon juice. But unfortunately, my father comes behind me, nips the nape of my neck and nods his head for me to follow Mason to our table.

"*Scusa, signorina,* my Piccolo, he is just a boy." As my father speaks to the beautiful woman, I crawl under the table humiliated.

Then a man who wears a white chef jacket approaches our table and chats amiably with Mason. He has a kind and humorous face, and when he bends down to scratch behind my ears, I do detect a whiff of scrod before he strolls back into the kitchen.

My father accustomed to fine dining has tucked his napkin under his collar and studies the wine list with interest. Mason studies the menu as intently, but shakes his head with a vehement, no. "I don't care how good they say it is, let's skip the *crudo*, I don't do raw. What do you say, Pops?"

"I say we begin with wine," he replies, being a great lover of the grape who for these long years has not had a sip. Mason, who does seem to know his way around this trattoria, motions for a man he calls George to join us who in response to our host's request recommends a Sicilian wine from Etna. From under the table, I hear my father's prompt and heartfelt assent. "Yes, yes, that will be fine. And please, two bowls for me and my son. Who will be joining us," he adds in a tone that means that I must obey.

Coming out from under the table, I take my place on a wooden chair beside my father and study the artwork on the wall, thinking that I could do much better than the framed splatters of color. But my thoughts soon refocus from art to food when our own charred octopus arrives on a long plate. The smell ravages my nostrils, and I want so badly to take it under the table and devour it alone, but remembering my manners, like my father I tuck my napkin under my collar and wait to be served. We then move smoothly from the antipasti to the cavatelli. But because I was brooding under the table, Mason has not yet ordered our second course.

"So, what it'll be, Sniff? I think I'll go for the fish, but it's a toss-up between the *spigola* and the *orata*." Both from the Mediterranean, I know them to be equally tasty, but his words seem distant to me as biting into a dumpling that pops with the triumvirate flavor of mozzarella, tomato and basil in my mouth, I can think of nothing else.

Mason motions for the server to come to our table, and to my great pleasure she does. Her name is Iona and for our second course, she suggests *pollo scarpariello*, but Mason explains that the pickled hot pepper in the dish might not agree with greyhounds—although I would have eaten rocks had they been recommended by this pert and pretty female.

I am aware that in the company of Americans such observations are highly inappropriate, so I do not speak them aloud, but instead think them to myself as I gently pant. Given the loveliness of her skin, soft and smooth as any greyhound, and the ever so slight mustiness that wafts from her armpits, I am wholly infatuated. So when she does suggest the *osso bucco*, my lips quiver and excitement rises through my body.

But given the smallness of the dining room and proximity of the tables, my tail—that I have kept politely slack, hanging from the back of my chair—goes wild, swatting the leg of an older woman who sitting at the nearby table laughs pleasantly. Her companion does not find it amusing, insisting that there are laws to restrict the presence of unruly service dogs from public places, but Mason comes to our defense.

"Listen, lady, these are no service dogs. You're looking at two old school Italian artists, and we're on our way to see this dog's first New York exhibition."

I hear the exchange but feel many miles away as I follow the retreating form of Iona with my eyes, particularly her well delineated haunches. As she disappears into the kitchen, I raise my snout and howl both in sadness for her leaving and anticipation of the veal shanks.

"I suppose that too is old school," says the woman with the taut face and puffy lips that hold no appeal.

Her partner, whose skin is a map of laugh lines and life experience, reaches over to stroke my chest. "Oh, Marie, loosen up. He's adorable." Her gesture is a poor substitute for what I at that moment desire, but it does calm down my wagging tail, and I lose the urge to howl.

"Perhaps you ladies would enjoy another bottle of wine." Mason motions for George.

"Oh, we couldn't," replies the prettier of the two. "We've had enough already."

"Nonsense, Maggie," interrupts Marie who shoots her partner the same look that she gives me before turning to the sommelier to discuss the wine list. With my sense of hearing heightened by the excellent acoustics in the dining room, I overhear her whisper to her partner. "What we don't drink, we'll take home."

The food to put it mildly far exceeds any dog dream of a meal. And having been so long away from my city's exquisite cuisine, subsisting on a mix of kibble and whatever tasty meat Mason has been throwing into a pot, I have longed for a bite of real Italian food.

And here on our little boat on the island of Manhattan, we dine in a manner to which we were accustomed back home in Venezia, where even a laborer or an artist eats like a king.

Then the braised veal shank arrives on a bed of risotto laced with morel mushrooms.

From the moment that Iona's lovely hand sets down the plate to when I am sucking the marrow from the bone and lapping up the last drops of gravy, I am in a sort of daze—as if my spirit hovers above my body, watching myself eat. But from what I see, I can say with certainty, it is a delightful meal.

Iona returns to our table to offer us desert, but my father and I decline, never having acquired a taste for sugar. Mason, however, orders a slice of *budino* which, being a rather large man, he consumes in several forkfuls. But how a plateful of pudding can hold his attention after an exquisite dish of seafood, I cannot comprehend.

"George!" Mason calls out over the crowd who seem to like to talk as much as they like to eat. "We'll take another bottle."

And when that bottle opens with a sleek pop, Mason fills our bowls, his glass and turns toward Maggie and Marie.

"I see you polished off that bottle, ladies," he says, pouring the last of our wine into their glasses. "Let me top you off." This time not only Maggie, but her friend Marie also giggles like a schoolgirl.

My father then raises himself up from his chair and warmed by the wine and the camaraderie of that dinner, he holds his bowl in two paws to the height of his chest and speaks in a sonorous voice that draws the attention of the diners at the nearby tables.

"My friends. And I call you my friends because since ancient times, we have been that. Tonight is a night of liberation, a new life, a new freedom. For me, for my son and our paesano, Mason Maldonado."

Now my father's words reach out and hush the din of that crowded dining room. "You do not know our story, though perhaps one day you will. But it is the story of all who toil on this earth and take pride in the products of their labor, who having made them deserve what is due all workers: respect and compensation. And for those who are forced to work without nature's rewards, food and sleep and dignity; for those who toil against their will around the world, beaten and spat upon and denied their birthrights—let us resolve to be intolerant."

My father then pauses to regain the attention of those diners who have been called back to their plates. "Yes, there I said it. Let us be intolerant, intolerant of captivity—for no male, no female, no offspring was born to be the property of another. Freedom for all," calls out my father raising his bowl high above his head as all the males, females and offspring in the dining room raise their glasses with us.

"Freedom for all," we sing out in one voice, and we drink deeply to the kinship of all species.

So moved am I with emotion, I nearly forget the purpose of our evening is to attend the exhibition at the Gallstone Gallery which is just around the block. So, tossing down my napkin, I step from my chair as two men, approximately the same height and equally well-dressed, rise from a nearby table. The one with silver hair nods toward Mason as the other polishes off his glass of wine.

"Hey, Harry, how's it going?" says Mason, then nodding toward the other gentleman, "Yo, Julian, what's up?"

A broad and bearded man, striking in his stature, nods in response and passing our table, rubs my head and then my father's before slipping out of the restaurant—a gesture I sometimes find patronizing, but at that moment I understand is intended by the stranger as one of appreciation for our species, and perhaps for my father's speech.

As they walk toward the door, I admire the cut of their jackets. "Who was that?"

"That's Harry Galoshian and Julian. Guy can't stand him."

"Artists?"

"Harry owns one of these joints around here, and Julian? Yeah, he's an artist. Sculptor, painter, film maker, he does it all. I just dropped ten bucks on a bootleg DVD of his, worth every dime."

With Guy Gizárd's credit card, Mason pays the bill and leaves a sizable tip as Iona smiles warmly and touches his arm—although I deeply wish that she had touched mine.

My eyes downcast I climb the wooden steps slowly toward the door, her smell rising above the rest—a tumult of scents from half eaten meals and uncorked bottles of wine, human breath and various colognes wrapped in the aroma of the seafood broiling, poaching, simmering in the kitchen. Reaching the top plank, I dare to turn around and see that with the gaze of a luminous Madonna from the brush of Bellini, Iona is looking back at me. I run to her and sit at her feet, aware only of her curling lips, good teeth and laughing eyes.

"You are so cute." The beautiful young female scratches me behind my ear. Although at this moment I am hoping for so much more, these things take time I tell myself, slightly tipsy from the wine.

"As are you."

"Come again," she says with a smile.

"Yes, I will." My tail wagging, I gaze deeply into her dark eyes. "I will, Iona. I will come again."

"Oh, so you remembered my name. You are a smart dog."

"I remember well what is important to me."

I sense many of their electronic toys pointed in our direction, and I resent the patrons ogling what should be respected as a private moment.

"Well, nice to meet you. And your name is?"

"Piccolo. Piccolo Fortunato."

"Well, Piccolo, I've got to get back to work."

"Yes, but please, one question."

"Sure, what is it?"

"Your name, Iona, what does it mean?"

"Iona? In Scotland it's an island, but in Hebrew it means dove."

"Ah, yes, an island dove."

But at this moment, no doubt jealous of the attention Iona is lavishing upon me, George the sommelier snaps his fingers and nods his head toward a table in the rear. I watch Iona walk away and make a silent vow that we will one day continue our conversation.

Very jovial now, the ladies from the adjacent table step outside to join us as we walk down the street, enjoying the cool breeze that blows off the Hudson.

"Let's go to the High Line," says Maggie echoed by Marie.

"What is this high line?"

"A park, just down the block."

"Park." My ears perking up, I think that a good run before viewing my work at the Gallstone Gallery will calm my nerves that the superb food and several bowls of wine have not completely quelled.

"Yeah, sure," says Mason who despite his enthusiasm has to stop three times while climbing the metal stairs up which Papa and I bound.

I reach the High Line first. "This is it?" With disappointment I see no green space to run, just a long walkway crowded with two cavalcades of people moving in opposite directions, some walking alone, some arm in arm, and others foolishly captivated by their devices unaware of the nearly full moon that shines behind the swiftly moving clouds.

The wind picks up and the grasses along the edges of the walkway chatter, and the yellow skirt of Maggie's sundress swells and flaps up toward her face. She laughs and forces the folds back down, but for that one moment, I admire her shapely legs and imagine how satisfying it would be to run alongside this strong female for many miles.

"Yeah, Sniff's right." Mason sits down on the only vacant bench in sight where I take a seat beside him. "You call this a park? The boardwalk at Coney Island's better, and there at least you got an ocean looking back at you."

"Yes," agrees Maggie, looking out over the river, her silver hair blowing about in the crisscrossing currents of air. "Brooklyn has always been better, but just look up at that gibbous moon. Isn't it gorgeous?"

"Yes, this moon phase," slurs Marie who sways and looks as if she might be blown away, "is a time to release old energies and welcome new wisdom."

Remembering my manners, I jump from the bench to offer her my seat. "Please, signora, sit."

"Grazie."

"And also time," says her friend Maggie with an angelic smile and a gentle burp, "to honor the goddess Trivia."

"Trivia?" I furrow my brow as a swallow dips before me to eat a fly midair. I watch as it darts upward toward a windowsill just beyond the High Line where it perches below the eaves.

"Small talk."

"No, Mason," says my father who has studied much. "It's from the Latin *trivium* which means a crossroad that branches out three ways. She was much honored in ancient times who with her dogs was the keeper of the cosmic soul and with her torch lit the way to lead lost travelers home."

"Don't listen to them, Sniff. They're all hammered."

"We may have drunk much wine, Mason, but we speak the truth." Then tilting his snout upward, Papa croons, "All hail to Trivia." A chant that is echoed by Maggie and Marie.

Then as the first rain drops splatter on the walkway, he leaps on the bench and holds out his pork pie hat toward the ladies who sway as he sings the Frank Sinatra classic, *Fly Me to the Moon.*

Though many passers-by are dispersing in the rain, several stop to sing along as does Mason who, though a natural baritone, can lift his voice into a surprisingly high upper register. His voice with Papa's rises above the rest, their last note resonating with the applause of the small, brave audience who have remained undeterred by the rumble of thunder rolling across the river.

"Okay," bellows Mason, rising from the bench. "Enough with the a cappella. We gotta get to the gallery."

Maggie and Marie shout good night, then holding hands, hurry down the stairway and run off in the rain while we take off toward the gallery. Lightning snaps illuminating the rooftops while a silver rivulet streams along the curb. With Mason huffing behind us, Papa and I slow down to trot beside him.

Mason is heaving, holding his chest with his open hand. "This is it." Light shines through the glass panels of the gallery's façade where Mason peers in. "Yo, there's Kibbleman," he says, catching his breath. "And that guy from New York magazine, what's his name? You know he used to drive a meat truck? You gotta love it. Oh, and there's that MOMA intern. It's those young ones Tweeting all the time that make Guy nervous. He must be sweating bullets."

"No need for violence." I raise my paw, knowing how quickly these Americans engage in gunplay.

"Yeah, well, last show they tore him up pretty bad. You know, sorry, pops," Mason says nodding toward my father, "but after he locked you up, he had one lousy intern after the next, and the reviews, well, they almost put him under."

"Guy was in the cellar?"

"Yeah. In terms of his career, more like in the dirt. This show's his chance to turn things around."

Most of what Mason is saying eludes me, but given the rain and my anxiety, I scratch at the door to enter the Gallstone Gallery and face whatever awaits us. Mason holds it open, and we enter. Inside my father starts shaking off the rain as all eyes turn toward us.

"Papa," I whisper. "Not here."

"Oh, sorry." Papa smiles awkwardly as a woman in a short black dress with knees like two rolled pork loins takes his picture. Beyond her I see *Sniff.* As in a dream, I approach. It stands over two meters tall, towering above me with its organic, triangulated form that embraces the space and invites the viewer into its world. In that moment I scan the gallery, blocking out all curious faces and see only my three sculptures and admire how *Sniff* and *Sill* and *Doom* command that open space.

My reverie is dashed as Gallstone strides toward us, her teeth bared. "Mason? And the interns," she utters softly with contempt, maintaining her false smile. "What the hell are you doing here?"

"We have come to view this exhibition of my son's sculpture."

"You have to leave." She takes her device from the small bag that she clutches. "And if you don't, I'm calling the police."

"No need for that, Gloria. Not all press is good press. Mason was just taking these dogs back to my studio, weren't you Mason?" he says with a steely glint in his eye as if threatening a boy with a belt.

"I'm not a kid anymore, Guy. As of tonight, I am my own man."

"Your own man? He says he's his own man." Guy shakes his head and laughs to the crowd that has gathered as the rain dribbles down the panes of glass behind him. "And these two mutts—what do you think, they own themselves too?"

Gloria nods toward the rear of the gallery. "Guy, you're drunk. Let's discuss this in my office."

"No, we're settling this right now." He raises his voice, addressing the crowd.

"These dogs claim that this exhibition is not the work of Guy Gizárd. That because I hired them as interns to fabricate my sculpture in my studio, that they somehow have a right to it. Is there an attorney here tonight?"

Several lawyers, I lose count at eight, step forward from the crowd while from the inner pocket of his jacket, Guy takes out two documents—one on which I had placed my paw print in the dining room of the *Preziosa,* and the other identical in text and in signature, the proud mark of the Fortunato family.

"Examine these," he orders, handing the documents to the gaggle of lawyers who pass them from hand to hand, nodding their heads in agreement.

A woman in a tight suit with a skirt so short she might as well have worn the jacket alone steps forward. "We concur. The work, in our opinion, belongs to Studio Gizárd. But litigation is advised."

Guy laughs maniacally and runs around the gallery, pointing at *Sniff* and *Sill* and *Doom.* "I own it. I own it. I own it." Then pointing at me and Papa, he adds, "and I especially own it and it—because your whole doggie dog existence depends on me, Guy Gizárd, you pretentious, low-class laborers."

I draw back, preparing to attack, but my father's foreleg blocks me.

"But, Papa, the insult."

"Wait."

"You mutts need me. You all need me because without me, without my art—what's your world? Empty and meaningless." As he shouts at the crowd, some of them nod and bleat like sheep, yes, he's right, while most of them are busy tapping on their devices.

Guy Gizárd coughs then points straight at me, and as he rants his eyes bulge, his cheeks grow bright and his body gives off a faint smell of salt and mud. "And you? You're a dime a dozen. I get twenty, thirty resumes a week from dog boys like you begging to work at Studio Gizárd, gratis, no charge, free labor and no perks. They get it. I'm the master, they're the interns. Like I told you on the ship, kid, without me, without my money, you're nothing, you are... no... body." Guy Gizárd's voice falters as he clutches his chest and falls heavily to the floor.

At that moment, every device in the gallery is raised, some calling for help while others take pictures of a body writhing on the floor that within moments is still—its mouth ajar, its eyes still open with a vague look of fear. In the face of death, the lawyers have dispersed, and a woman pushes through the crowd who begins to breathe into the open mouth and pump hard on the chest.

"It is too late," my father whispers. "He is already gone."

"Dead?"

"Yes, son, when you were about to attack, I had already sensed death stalking him. And once death has entered a room, it rarely leaves without the life it has come to claim."

"I smelled it."

"Like the lagoon at low tide on a hot summer day. Before the sea water returns, that is the smell of death."

Mason is beside the body now, wailing like a boy who has lost both his parents. The siren of the ambulance approaches and its blue lights lash the white walls of the studio. And at that moment, my sculpture has no meaning for me.

As they lift the body from the cold floor onto the gurney, my father licks its hand.

"Why?"

"Out of pity."

"Why pity him, Papa, after what he did to us?"

"When death comes, life need not be over. For the kind-hearted, the generous, no matter how imperfect we have been, death is as simple as leaving the cinema and pushing open the glass door into the street and heading home. But for those who live to feed their greed and appetite at the expense of other beings, that soul will suffer torments that far exceed the pain inflicted—and that death will far exceed the single day we spend on the face of earth."

I lower my head as Papa introduces me to the knowledge that visited him in that dark Morgan Avenue cellar. "Yes, I licked that hand that hurt me because I pity the poor soul."

Mason approaches us, his bloated face pale and his eyes bloodshot. "The doc says it's for sure. Guy's gone."

"Yes," my father says, "I know."

"We gotta go, they're locking up."

My father nods toward the body on the floor. "We should go with him."

"Gloria's sending one of her interns to handle it. We might as well head home."

In silence we drive back to Brooklyn, the sound of the rain that has fallen plashing under the tires. We cross the bridge to

Williamsburg, but I feel no joy as we turn down these now familiar streets—not even when we wait at a stop sign for the pretty girl to pass. Her bare shoulder swirls with rosebuds and pink petals, and so beautifully she smiles, as pointing at me she says to her male companion, "A greyhound, look."

"It's a whippet," says the young man with a gaping hole in the lobe of his ear.

"Really?" The female continues to stare over her lovely shoulder, still smiling.

"Yes, I'm sure," he insists as they cross the street. "I can tell by the length of the muzzle."

As we turn down Morgan Avenue, the rain falls heavily again, the car windows rise, and I cannot help but wish it had been me with her instead of him, and how instead of quibbling over details, I would spend our time together nuzzling her neck.

The wipers tap out their sad, monotonous dirge as Mason pulls up in front of the building. With a click he makes the steel door rise and pulls in off the street. We enter the building where under the light bulb in the hallway, Mason's bulging eyes glisten. He pulls down the lever to open the cage-like doors of the freight elevator which we ride together. "You don't mind if I stay upstairs with you guys, do you? I mean just until tomorrow."

"Of course, Mason. When a friend asks, there is no tomorrow."

"Thanks, Pops. For everything. And I am really sorry, you know, for the way things went."

"What's done is done, my friend. And it's only those who do nothing who make no mistakes." My father rubs his muzzle against his hand as step from the elevator.

"Well, I gotta get some shut-eye." Mason looks around the studio for a place to lay down his big body. "Oh, yeah, no beds up here, huh?"

I nod toward my thick blanket in the corner. "It's really quite comfortable."

"Well, I slept on air mattresses before, how bad can it be?"

With a thud, he lowers himself to the floor. "But what about you guys?"

"For us, Mason, this night is not for sleeping."

I cross the studio to where several weeks before I had roughed out the sculpture from the log of cherry wood. And there I untie my tool roll from which I choose two chisels as my father takes two mallets from the shelf. Throughout that night we carve side by side until a pale gray light slides over the rooftops and water towers of Brooklyn and into the studio where we step back and wag our tails in approval of our finished work of art.

I name the work Iona—Iona in honor of the islands of Venezia and the islands of this city, but most of all in honor the lovely Iona, the island dove who served us so well at the Chelsea trattoria the night before, and who one day I would meet again.

For several weeks we remain at the Morgan Avenue studio as clearly Mason needs companionship after the sudden death of Guy Gizárd. I am surprised at how he grieves this man for whom I feel no pity, but clearly their relationship of many years had been deep and complex. The body is cremated, and the box of ashes kept on a shelf in Mason's room on the first floor until a brief memorial service is held after the opening of the Gauntley Biennial where our work *Iona* is well received.

Intermezzo

Generously Mason has paid for our passage on the *Preziosa* with a sizable reserve of cash he calls his kitchen money and given Papa several hundred dollars for when we arrive back home, an amount that Papa insists he will repay as soon as he reestablishes his studio in Venice.

That morning after the service, Mason drives us to Pier 94 where our ship is set to sail. On the seat beside me is the cedar box with an engraved bronze tag, bearing the artist's name by birth, Gerald Gizzard.

"Mason, what will you do?" my father asks as Mason parks the jeep.

"After I drop you guys off, I'm driving up to Guy's place in the Adirondacks. I know that's where he'd wanna be." Mason takes the key from the ignition and for a few minutes we sit without speaking. "Yeah, well, he left me the cabin with a couple acres. I'll spend some time up there, you know, to think. And then who knows, maybe I'll stop by Venice and drink some wine and eat cicchetti with a couple of paesan." Mason climbs out of the jeep and crosses to open the passenger door for my father. Meanwhile, smelling new adventure in the moist sea air, I leap onto the sidewalk and drag my duffel bag down to the cement.

"Oh, by the way, I got a text from a Gloria, she says she lined up a buyer, some guy from Singapore, wants that cherry piece."

"Mason, after all this, how can you even ask?"

"Yo, pops, listen to me. According to the contract, only the steel work belonged to Guy. *Iona* is yours."

"*Iona* will be returning home to Venice with us."

"You sure? You guys can make buku bucks off that piece."

"That piece, Mason, is worth much more than money."

"I get it, and don't worry. I'll make sure she gets home safe." Mason squats down and holds my father's muzzle between his two fat hands and kisses it loudly. Then he turns to me and does the same.

"It's show time, boys." And without his usual gusto, Mason gets back into the jeep and wipes his eyes with the sleeve of his blazer. "This sun is murder," he says reaching for his sunglasses on the dashboard along with two slim boxes that he hands down to us. We open them to find two pairs of eye shades identical to his own. "I figured you might need them on the ship." Papa and I both lick the hand that dangles out the window. "And this way when you put them on, you'll think of me."

"We will think of you often and with kind thoughts, my good friend."

"And yo, Sniff," he says reaching into his pocket. "You almost forgot this." In his many-ringed fingers he holds out my yellow welding cap, the one I had worn the first night I met with Guy Gizárd. "You left it on your workbench."

"Thanks, Mason," I reply putting on my cap. "For everything."

"Yeah, for everything, little guy," says Mason as he pushes a button on the dashboard, releasing the notes of that soulful tune that Charles Mingus composed in honor of his own good friend, Lester Young.

"So long, Sniff. And goodbye pork pie hat," he calls, pulling away from the curb into the southbound flow of traffic, the music spilling out the open windows of the jeep as he drives away.

I hoist my duffel bag of tools onto my back and with Papa by my side, I board the ramp of the *Preziosa* an older and a wiser dog. But as we have no way of letting Mama know we are returning home, for the first time I can see how useful their devices might be after all.

The small flames of light on the water are burning my eyes, so

I put on the dark shades that say Revo and stand on the deck to watch the harbor pass us by—the green lady, the skyline, the memories both harsh and kind recede with the shoreline until we are fully out to sea.

My father comes to stand my side. "You have been very quiet, my son."

"Yes, I have been replaying the story of our passage to America, so I will not forget a single detail when we tell Mama."

"Yes, my Piccolo, your mother, my Biscotti, she has always loved a good story."

4 Return to the Cosmos

I am standing on the upper deck when after two weeks at sea, the Preziosa sails across the lagoon toward the slip of San Basilio. It is here I first met Guy Gizárd, the man who briefly called himself my master—until summoned by his own to sweat and labor as an unpaid intern of the cosmos. There I hope he is gaining as much wisdom as I did in the cellar of his Williamsburg studio.

And that the heat of the vindaloo is to his liking.

Barely six months have passed since that morning in the crowded bàcaro when I first told Mama my intention to go and find Alfonso. Yet since then, the sights, the sounds, the smells, the tastes both good and evil have penetrated my being, saturating my senses with particles of experience that like amino have linked to form the proteins that feed my soul.

I am no longer a pup.

I am Piccolo the full-grown male, not only in my physical being but in my mind.

Now I can feel the gears whizzing in my brain, the rumble of invention, the sparks flying as one thought engenders the next with ideas for new artworks exceeding the pages in my journal.

In my notebook I sketch a quick impression of the approaching shoreline—the tiled rooftops, domes and spires of Venice where atop the Customs House, the Goddess Fortuna balances on a golden ball. In one hand she holds an oar and in the other a sail, spinning with the same shifting winds that have brought us home.

Papa approaches, setting down the clanking duffel bag with our tools. Looking out at Venice, he takes off his pork pie hat with a sweeping gesture and holds it over his heart. “Buongiorno, bella

Venezia."

"Yes," I agree with a wag, "she is beautiful."

Stepping from the deck, I feel the same anticipation that followed me from Pier 94 in New York City nudge me through the throng of passengers and down the ramp. My legs wobble as I cross the wooden footbridge toward the Zattare where the wet stones of the promenade reflect a pearl gray sky.

"Wait here, I'll be right back," says Pappa who surrounded by tourists needs to find a more private place to pee. Trotting west, he passes the sculpture of three musicians. He barks and points toward them—one on cello, two playing violins—bent with the force of their combined notes frozen in time.

"Nice bronze, eh, son? But we'll do better."

I reply with two sharp yaps as he disappears behind its round stone base.

My nose twitching, I inhale that distinct aroma that is Venice and realize that during my many months of artistic labor in Williamsburg, suffering both unbridled deceits and wild joys, I had not thought of her.

Not even once.

And now angered by neglect, she strikes me in the muzzle with the full force of her being. Drawn to her dirt, I sniff between the roots of a nearby tree, my nostrils quivering, overpowered by the cross currents of her smells—no, not smells but layers of her energy that like centuries of patina have been creeping over the surfaces of my city.

Venice.

My Venice.

I stand still and breathe more deeply to discern each layer—the smell of diesel from the ship, offset by the interlacing aromas of fresh bread, coffee and cacao wafting from the *pasticceria.* And shifting beneath them, the lagoon itself—its cleansing blend of water, salt and mud mixing with the remnants of a hundred thousand meals that with each acqua alta rise, bubbling up through

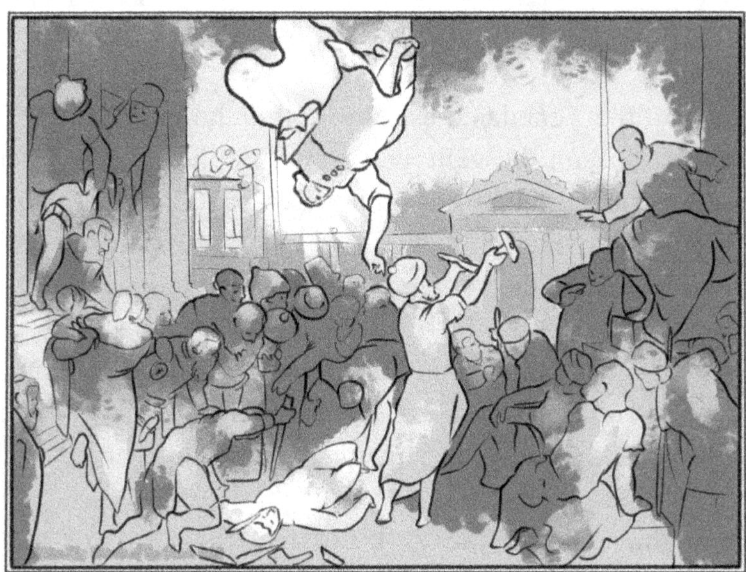

Tintoretto Miracle of the Slave 1548

manhole covers, spilling over doorsills, slowly rendering sheds and palaces alike into watery museums for crabs and fish and prawn.

Moist and blue, I feel the molecules of air streaming down my throat into the channel of my chest that fills with each inhalation.

And then I bolt. Gaining speed, I run along the edge of Dorsoduro with the sky and clouds and early morning strollers all a blur, the water splashing up along the walkway dousing my legs. With a sharp turn I am running through the narrow streets, down alleys and over bridges—but always moving toward the Grand Canal, the artery through which flows the lifeblood of Venice.

Then something deep inside of me says, sit. And so, I sit and feel a wave of antiquity wash over me through the open door of the Gallerie dell'Accademia. Beside me stands an old man in a blue uniform who chews on the stub of a short, unlit cigar.

"Welcome back, Piccolo," he says, displaying his ochre-colored teeth.

"Buongiorno," I reply but am too overwhelmed with the emotion of my homecoming to strike up a conversation. Inside the cashier and the other guards also smile, recognizing me perhaps as the pup who each Saturday used to sit at his mother's paws, reading the adventures of Tintin while she sketched and painted miniatures of the Venetian masters to sell in the Piazza.

I move through the galleries, drawn by the scent of each era preserved in the pigment of its paints. Led back in time to a musky age when men rarely bathed, in the brushstrokes of the Renaissance, I smell the complex aroma of egg tempera, turpentine and wine.

Here I stand before a dark and brooding painting that frightened me as a pup. It is *The Miracle of the Slave* by Tintoretto whose force and energy as a painter, rightfully earned him the name, Il Furioso.

From the looming canvas I can feel the terror of the man pinned to the ground by his torturer, surrounded by the gawking mob. But look again, and I feel only triumph as the spirit of San Marco swoops down to rescue him. There he hovers above the scene, his robes flapping when without a fight the implements of torture are broken—the hammers and the splintered spikes with which they would have gouged out the man's eyes are rendered useless by the saint.

"The only true masters are the masters of their craft," says my father, noisily setting down our duffel bag on the marble tiles.

"Papa." I gasp, realizing I left him and our tools unattended on the pier.

"No problem, son. I knew where to find you."

"It's good to be back. But somehow it all looks different."

"Each time we return, we see with new eyes. Like this one. Before I left Venice, I understood it as a painting. But after being locked up in that cellar, I now feel the painting here." Papa strikes his chest.

Being reminded how long my father was imprisoned in that Brooklyn studio and thrown into that cellar to rot, I feel a low growl rise and churn between my jaws.

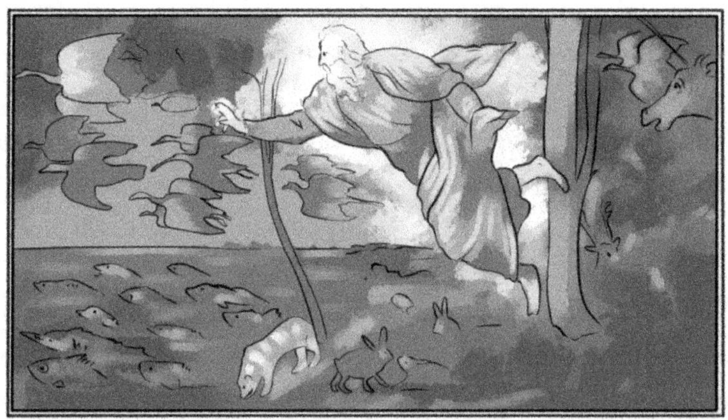

Tintoretto Creation of the Animals 1550

"You are right to be angry," says Papa, sotto voce. "For Nature creates no one to be the object of another. But now is not the time."

I mask my anger behind one of their grins—until a woman chewing gum exclaims between snaps. "Oh, look at the puppy. Isn't it the cutest thing!"

When I snarl, her oddly plucked eyebrows rise, and she hurries from the gallery.

"Come," says Papa. "Let us visit another by our good friend, Tintoretto."

Hauling our bag of tools, I cross into the adjoining gallery to view the *Creation of the Animals*. On this canvas, Il Furioso has painted a luminous god, ushering the fish and birds into being. On shore are the tetrapods, including one curious canine ancestor who sniffs at the edge of the water.

I study the seafood, and then follow Papa into the early Renaissance room, wishing I had eaten more from the breakfast buffet tables on the ship. Entering this space, I feel serenity surrounded by the Madonnas of Bellini, the softness of their gaze matched by the celestial folds of their blue mantles.

"Piccolo, over here." Papa calls for me to join him before a painting of Saint George and the dragon.

"Ah, Mantegna. Did you know Piccolo that he was Bellini's brother-in-law?"

"Yes, Papa." I nod as Mama has taught me much about the pedigree of the families of our city and the creative rivalry between these in-laws that pushed the family business to great heights of success.

"Me, I go for Mantegna. Bellini came from money, but Andrea was the son of a carpenter, made his own way in the world. Like us, eh, son?"

Like Papa I am proud that we come from a long line of self-made artists—like Tintoretto and Giovanni Battista Tiepolo, who few know in early life suffered dire poverty after his own father's death. Yet still I would welcome a little wealth and a well-equipped studio—a desire I feel more sharply as I gaze up at this painting of a young man splendidly dressed in gleaming armor at whose feet the dragon lies dead with the jagged end of a broken spear protruding from his mouth.

"Much can be learned from Mantegna," says Papa. "Here he expresses the triumph of the saint and the agony of the sinner."

Strongly I feel otherwise—that the painting conveys the power of those who wield the weapons, who having slain the innocent make them appear to be the monsters. There is something in the empty eyes of the dragon that saddens me—and in the fruit that hangs above Saint George's halo that intensifies my hunger. With my stomach rumbling, I follow Papa across the gallery to where a tourist takes a picture of my mother's favorite painting, *The Tempest* by Giorgione.

With stripes of red, white and blue crisscrossing her fingernails, she holds her device aloft, a broad smile stretching her thin lips.

When she snaps what they call a selfie, the guard appears with finger raised, scolding, "No photo!"

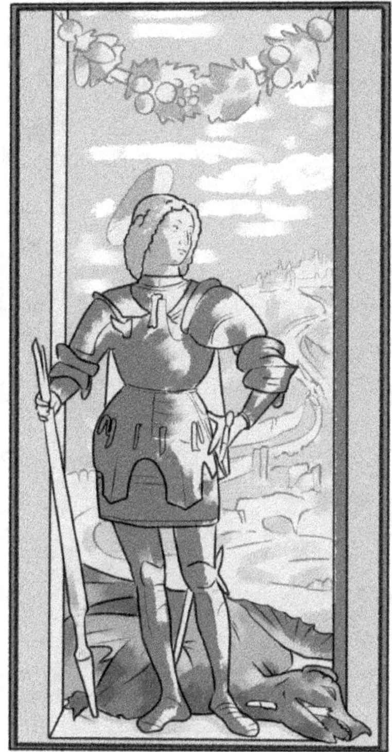

Andrea Mantegna Saint George 1460

The young woman, pretty but ill bred, makes a sound by snapping her tongue against her teeth. “Really? Like it’s such a big deal.” With her sandals loudly flip-flopping, she departs while we three exchange the glance that our ancestors have shared ever since the days when the barbarians drove us from mainland to live on the lagoon. Our eyes meet, our shoulders shrug and with a communal smirk, we shake our heads.

“Americans,” the guard mutters and returns to his post, leaving us alone to admire Giorgione’s *bella donna.* Looking up at the child suckling on the teat of this female who sits on the bank of the stream, I feel the contentment of a pup.

Yet as an artist, I take a step back to study the composition. On the left is a passing figure, a male whose gaze creates a line across the canvas to the seated nude while far above them in the

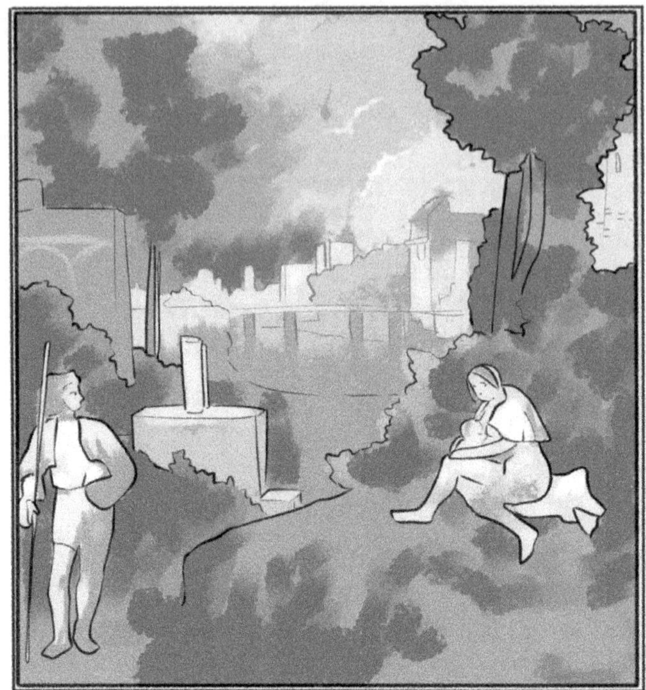

Giorgione The Tempest 1506

distance a bolt of lightning slits the sky, as dark as the waters of the canal. From the doorway, Papa gives a quick yap to draw my attention from the canvas. I follow him outside the museum where we make our way through the swarming tourists and stop at the open door of a bàcaro. Beside us, an old man places a broom of twigs into a dented cart.

The rubbish collector enters, followed by an old dog whose black muzzle is flecked with silver and whose lumbering movements suggest many years of hard labor.

"Come, son. You must be hungry," says Papa who approaches the glass counter where stands a broad-shouldered man with a firm jaw and large ears edged with odd patches of fur.

"Fortunato. It's been a long time. Good to see you again, old friend!"

"And you, too, Gian Carlo."

"You must have a story to tell, eh, Alfonso?"

"And then some, my friend, but the stories will have to wait, eh?" Papa wags his tail as he orders cicchetti and two bowls for our wine. When Gian Carlo sets down the small plates, Papa's eyes widen, his brow lifts and he inhales deeply, admiring the baby octopus lightly dressed in lemon juice and olive oil. "Ah, my *folpeti*," he says with as much affection as if they are his children.

And with eyes half-closed as when he sings of love, his lids quiver, and he takes a bite. All is silent for a moment, then he nudges the plate of fried meatballs toward me. "Eat," he commands and gladly I obey. With each chew the intercourse of meat and spices fills my mouth with an unspeakable pleasure that is only heightened by the wave of white wine that courses down my gullet. Our snack consumed, Papa peels back the Velcro strip that seals the side pocket of our duffel bag and reaches for his wallet. But with a wave of his thick hand, Gian Carlo refuses payment. "No, Alfonso, today you don't pay."

My father thanks him, and after lapping up the last drops of wine, we move toward the door where the old dog stands, looking out toward the canal where the water is a deep and pensive blue. I can hear the splash of a gondolier's oar as he rows beneath the bridge with two overweight tourists lounging on cushions. He points toward a random rooftop and is telling the couple in passable English that Marco Polo once occupied that room.

"And from that window Marco, he looks with his, eh, how do you say, the long glass to China."

"That's spy glass," drawls the man, correcting the boatman's English. "And he couldn't have seen quite that far."

The three chins of the female beside him jiggle with laughter at his weak joke. Then she raises herself on an arm as wide as a roast beef, her big shirt billowing and tilts her phone in our direction, nearly tumbling over the side.

"Sit," the gondolier commands while howling with amusement, we hurry over the bridge. Winding our way through courtyards and alleys, we bypass the legions of invaders that we

Venetians do our best to avoid as we go about our daily business.

Ah, the Piazza—how happy I am to set my paws down on the paving stones, so happy that I dive into a dense flock of pigeons devouring the crumbs off the body of a zealous tourist who has lain down on the ground with his arms outstretched. With a great flapping of wings, they rise as I jump over the young man whose jeans and t-shirt are splattered with their droppings, then run toward the spot near the Basilica where Mama has always parked the cart and set up her easel.

A breeze carries her scent to me—the scent of warm flesh, milk and kindness. Like a pup crazed with love for the mama, I pick up speed, plowing through tourists and growling at those who don't step aside fast enough. By my side, Papa does the same until we both stop short in front of a young mother, her blouse undone with an infant suckling hungrily at her breast. Her mouth opens and her eyes pop, seeing Papa and me bounding out of the crowd toward her. As she stumbles back, her baby turns its head to look at us, and sensing no danger, gurgles and laughs, milk trickling from the corners of its pink lips.

My father places a paw on his chest and raises the other to indicate we mean no harm as the mother spreads her lace shawl over its head, and a policeman approaches shouting.

"Signora, stop immediately. What you are doing is inappropriate!"

"On the contrary," Papa replies. "What she is doing is quite appropriate."

"For your kind, maybe. But not for us, and not in front of church property!"

"Is this not a house of God?"

"Yes."

"Then the landlord of this property would welcome her, considering his son was fed by our mother in the same way."

"Our mother?" the *Carabiniere* snorts and turns to the woman whose pale cheeks blush. "You have to use the public gardens, you can't feed your baby here. Please leave. And you too!" The young woman hurries off as my father loudly curses the retreating officer.

"Only an idiot would chase the Madonna and child from their own doorstep."

Twice we circle the Piazza, thinking perhaps Mama has moved her cart to a new spot. But we both know that if she had caught the faintest whiff of us, she would have run to find us. Clearly, she is not in the Piazza this morning, and so we decide to walk to the old neighborhood. Turning toward the Canale di Cannaregio, we approach the crumbling yellow building where Isabella had rented our ground floor room.

Papa knocks on the door and then winces with pain as a chunk of loose plaster from the façade strikes his head and crumbles on the pavement. But when the knob of the door jiggles, my heart races—but then stops when the landlady, a middle-aged woman with a gaunt face and whiskered chin, opens and stares at us with disdain.

"We are looking for a tenant of this building, Isabella, my wife."

"No dogs here," she snaps and slams the door as another chunk of plaster falls, this time bouncing off my head to the ground.

Papa and I look at one another in bewilderment—but where is Mama?

"*La chiesa*," says Papa.

We hurry down the Strada Nuova toward the square and honest building where Mama used to take me every Sunday morning for Mass. We climb the four steps and go into the entranceway where out of habit I dip my paw into the bowl of water and bless my myself as Mama trained me. The church is as I remember it, with a cool white light flowing through the circular window above the altar. We look around but Mama is not here.

"Ah, Piccolo. Your mother and I chose this church for its simplicity, the same simple design of the universe, the same design that we wanted for our life together."

I know the Chiesa San Felice is where he and Isabella married, and I watch him take off his hat and bow toward the same altar where I used to trip over my altar boy's cassock and sneeze at the smell of the incense.

"But, Papa, how come you never came in with us?"

"Because I have my own religion—with no priest, no Pope, no collection plate. And there is only one prayer."

"What is that?"

Raising a paw upward, he utters one word—grazie. Then lowering his paw toward the marble tiles, he speaks to the earth and the water below us—grazie. And then smiling he touches my brow and says—grazie.

And in return, I howl my gratitude for my father and mother, and the fathers and mothers who gave birth to them and am still howling back to the beginning of time and to our creator, when a priest hurries from the sacristy and points angrily toward the door through which we make a quick retreat.

We hurry down the Strada Nuova back toward the Piazza where this time as we approach through the shifting mobs of people, I see her easel and Mama sitting there painting, appearing and disappearing between the passers-by like a hesitant ghost.

"Mama!"

Slowly she stands. Her eyes glistening, she sneezes with great emotion as we run to her—the bells of San Marco ringing out, celebrating, or so it seems, our reunion.

"Alfonso!"

"Biscotti!"

"Mama!"

"Piccolo!"

Our voices blend into a joyous chorus. How inexpressible is what we feel at this moment as four puppies leap at our legs, wagging their tails wildly, not sure what is the source of this great happiness, but being puppies, quick to join in.

"Mama, Mama," they cry. "Who are the big males, Mama?"

With the last bell tolling from the Campanile, time stops in the square.

And with it, a moment's cessation of our hearts.

Then sharply Alfonso turns and runs. When my mother stands, I see that she does so with effort. "Alfonso, wait!" Reaching for the cane that is leaning against her easel, she says, "I must go after him. Piccolo, watch my babies."

Her babies? My brothers, my sisters?

"Mister, mister," three of them call, jumping at my legs. "Do you have candy, mister? We got shots today, hey mister, you got candy?"

I look down at them, various shades of tan and black and grey, each with a different jawline, one wide, one narrow, one pushed in like a pug. Three pups of mixed breeds united in that they are, I realize at this moment, my siblings. And now too I want to run from the square, but I cannot help but yield to my mother's wish.

"Who are you, mister?" they call out while nipping at my legs and the tip of my tail.

"Call me Zio Piccolo." And I lead them back to the cart where two tourists who wear striped shirts and tattered jeans admire my mother's artwork. The sun glints off the metal bars and rings that stud their faces as they ask many questions which in a daze I answer, as well as those of many tourists who stop at the cart that afternoon. Some are knowledgeable of painting, others looking in the wrong place for a cheap postcard. Then there are those who want only to snap a photo with me who in their eyes is as rare as a Babylonian.

"Zio, I'm hungry. Zio, play. Zio, he bit me!" The voices of the pups are indistinguishable—all pleading, all whining, all hungry—except for the one who creeps under the cart to stare at me through the spokes of the wheel.

"Who's that?"

"That's Aldo. He's always like that."

Something in his dark moist eyes and his creased brow draws me toward him. In appearance the other big-pawed pups with rough coats and shaggy tails have clearly been drawn from different genetic lines. Yet somehow, I feel that the one they call Aldo and I are the same.

"Aldo's oldest, but he's the littlest," the other pups taunt. "Littlest, littlest, Aldo is the littlest."

I approach the cart and bend close to the ground.

"Hey, little guy."

"Little?" he snaps back at me. "I am three months old. I am already weaned!"

How much this pup Aldo reminds me of me.

"Yes," I say in a serious tone. "But always remember, in small barrels, there's good wine."

"Where is my mother? And who is the male she calls Alfonso?"

"Truly, if I am your Zio Piccolo, you may call him zio too."

Aldo stares without blinking. "Where did you come from?"

"We have just returned from a long journey, and being fond of Isabella your mother, we came to pay our respects."

Clearly the other pups with thick haunches favor one side of their family, but Aldo with his sleek coat and long, thin legs is beyond the shadow of a doubt a descendant of greyhounds.

"A journey where?" chime in the other pups.

"A journey, *bambini*, that led us to the town of Soho—which in no way rivals our own Venice, but does have a reputation for displaying art."

"And where is this town?" asks Aldo crawling from under the cart to sit closest by my side.

"Across the sea in the district of Manhattan in the City of York they call New."

"Tell us, Zio, tell us, tell us," the bigger pups yap and leap, nipping each other and rolling on the ground.

"Yes, Zio, do," says Aldo, settling down at my feet as for the first time I recreate the tale, dear reader, that now unfolds before you on the pages in your hand or shines up at you from the screen of your device.

I tell of the ship, of the leash and the hot dog. The part about the biting down, the snap of the casing that tightly encloses the meat, the taste of its spices and the sweet tang of the relish, this they clamor for me to tell again and again—until I spot Isabella and Alfonso crossing the Piazza, a universe between them.

All but Aldo run to her begging for candy. He comes closer and motions for me to bend down to better hear the words he whispers in my ear.

"I like you, Zio Piccolo. I like you very much."

"And I like you, Aldo. And I'll tell you something else. I think that you and I will be great friends."

My father gives a single sharp bark which I know means I must follow. My mother comes to me and nuzzles my ear, without words conveying her great love as well as her thanks for watching her unruly litter. She then turns from me and licks the head of Aldo over and over while I back away from her, then bolt from the Piazza.

I find my father at the edge of the quay where he stands looking out at the leaden sky where the sun is no more than a small white plate behind a grey cloud.

"Papa."

"I blame myself."

"I don't understand."

"She begged me to stay. She whined, she sneezed, she gave me those long sad looks, and what did I do? The voice of my ego drowned out her pleas. Had I stayed, none of this would have happened."

He sighs deeply, lies down and places his head on his paws. I sigh and settle down beside him. In a daze, he speaks not to me, but to an indifferent sky.

"She struggled. First to keep our place in Cannaregio for my homecoming, and then to keep her son's hope alive that I would return at all. And then one day he too left. He left to find me. And alone she pushed the cart to the Piazza, then one afternoon there was disaster. Dragging that heavy cart, she tripped and broke her femur in two places. Yes, she received care from the local vet, but she had to pay him her week's earnings, and so hobbled home without the rent. And then when she could not work, waiting for her leg to heal, the landlady put her out."

"The witch." I growl recalling the old woman's scrawny leg beneath loose stockings that I could have snapped with one bite.

"She threw out all her belongings on the street, and your mother, too ashamed to even tell her sister of her abandonment by me, slept at night in the cart."

A sigh heaves from my chest and with it the realization that I too had left her.

"Alone and unprotected in a city of strangers who move through our streets like hungry ghosts. And where was I? In a filthy cellar in a distant land, insignificant as a mite."

We sigh again, and now he is no longer my father nor I his son—we are equals in grief and regret, and I feel our world shift.

All day we lie side by side—three huddled masses on the quay—two dogs and a duffel bag of useless tools. All night we stare into the dark waters of the Grand Canal edged with the amber glow from streetlights. All night I lie their motionless until I smell her approach and hear the tap of her cane and the patter of eight small paws, a cloud of sound around her.

"Mama, mama, we're tired, mama, we want to go home."

"Hush puppies."

"But, mama, we're hungry." They whine more loudly as they approach our bench.

"Alfonso, you can't stay out all night. The boy, Alfonso, you know he has sinus problems. Please," she begs.

Alfonso lifts his head and lets it drop again.

Mama waves her basket before us. I smell wicker and I smell

linen and wafting from within I smell the *baccalà mantecato*—the hard, dried cod soaked and beaten back to life, revived with sips of olive oil and reincarnated into a frothy new life on slices of Mama's fried polenta. Then she walks to a nearby bench to which I cannot help but follow. She takes off her shawl and spreads it on the damp slats of wood for the pups to sit and eat the snacks she has prepared. I am disoriented by the disparity of the perfection of the food and the disaster of our homecoming.

"Sit by me," she says, holding a tasty morsel before me. I accept and chew thoughtfully. "What is it, son? What's on your mind?"

"It's just that I don't understand any of this."

"Oh, Piccolo, life holds more complications than any of us can comprehend."

"But, Mama, a mixed breed?"

And the moment I have blurted out these words and see her expression as if a boot has kicked her in the chest, I regret them.

Then the hurt in her eyes, shifts to anger.

"That mixed breed has a name. And although he does not speak like you and I, Giuseppe is a loving and a loyal dog."

"I'm sorry. As long as he is a good husband and a good father."

"He is not my husband, nor is he their father."

Now the boot has struck me with such force that I am speechless.

And even as I recount these events, an old dog looking back on hard times, I wish my voice had not returned to me that night, for when I did speak it was those words that form my second regret in life.

"Mama, how could you?"

She pauses and stares, retaining her dark secret for one last moment before she reveals it to me. "It was not by choice, but by force."

My brain hums and my body clenches with rage. A low growl

rumbles from my chest as I bare my teeth. "I'll kill him."

"How do you kill a shadow, with what blade can you slit the throat of a memory?" And bowing her head, she says, "Forgive me, son."

"Mama, there is nothing to forgive, only to avenge."

"If I smell him in a dark alley, I will rip out his throat," she replies, softly growling so that the pups do not hear. "Just know, it was this dog that you dismiss as a mixed breed who took me to his owner's house, and in the shed beside it, brought me a clean blanket and a box in which I gave birth to this litter of pups, and for that I will always be grateful."

The pups are now splashing on the wet stones of the quay, fighting over a half-chewed heal of bread.

"That's enough," says Mama firmly. "Now get in the basket, we're going home."

The basket now empty, the wet pups climb in and snuggle under the crumb covered linen. All but Aldo who remains on the bench beside me. With his furrowed brow and the look in his eyes dark and deep, I realize he has been listening to our conversation, but doubt a three-month-old could possibly have understood.

My mother moves toward Alfonso and speaks to him as firmly as she has spoken to her pups. "And you must put aside the self-pity and follow me to the warm, dry place I have secured for you."

"With his money."

"I pay the landlord with my own earnings, much as I used to pay our rent," she says with an edge of anger that undercuts my father's unkindness.

"No. I will sleep here."

"And I will stay with Papa."

"Alfonso, do you want Piccolo to die of pneumonia? Stop being stubborn. Now get up."

Aldo stands on the bench by my side with two paws on my shoulder. "Mama is right. Come home with us." He licks my ear and adds, "brother."

Truly Aldo is an old soul, and I carry him home along with the bag of tools slung over my back, following Alfonso who follows Isabella along the Riva degli Schiavoni toward Castello. There at the water's edge stands the Arsenale, the ancient shipping yard where in better days the three of us had gone to see art exhibitions. Now as we pass, the irony strikes me that beyond these gates in 2001 my father had exhibited his own sculpture at the Biennale. The theme that year had been the Plateau of Humanity, yet since that time Alfonso had suffered at the base of humanity, tortured in that Williamsburg basement.

I say nothing of this as we three shadows move through the silent streets. When we come to a brick shed that leans against a small house, Isabella knocks on the door that hangs loosely in its frame. After a moment it creaks open, and someone barks a short greeting. As we enter, I recognize him by the glints of silver that encircle his muzzle. He is the old dog that I had seen that morning gazing out of the bàcaro at the canal, the same dog who had entered with the rubbish collector. But despite the look in his eyes that speaks of an ongoing struggle, this dog has power in his haunches and moves with the confidence of many hard-won battles.

Giuseppe nods toward the loft where my mother has laid out fresh blankets, but my father keeps his head down and his eyes fixed on the hard-packed earthen floor. Leaving the duffel bag in the corner by the stove, I climb the narrow planks behind my father to the pinewood platform from where I can see the pups leap on Giuseppe, yapping to him in his own language and speaking to our mother in hers.

"That's enough excitement for tonight," chides Isabella clapping her paws. "Now all of you, say goodnight and off to bed."

"Goodnight, Zio Piccolo, goodnight, Zio Alfonso," they shout in a chorus.

All except Aldo who drags his blanket to the far corner of the shed beside an old record player where he circles, pawing at the tattered woolen folds then calls out, "Goodnight, brother."

"Goodnight, Aldo."

A storm has blown off the lagoon and pelts the window with heavy droplets of rain throughout the night. Who could sleep after the revelations of that day? Certainly not Alfonso who paces, paces, paces, his obsessive steps echoing my own obsessive thoughts: why, why, why and how? How could this disaster have been averted? Finally, this trembling tower of repetitive thought collapses, and under the rubble I fall asleep. Not until a pale light filters through the newspapers taped to the small round window that overlooks the street, do I awake. Beside me the blanket on which my father has not slept is folded in a corner of the loft, and he is gone. Below I hear the early morning noises of a family stirring.

My mother shuffles in her slippers to where the three pups sleep in a tangle of legs and tails and tucks their blankets more snugly around them. Then moving toward a small gas range, she strikes a match and puts a flame under the iron pot. From a cannister she scoops out the yellow grain, and when the water begins to boil, she adds the polenta as the voice of Tony Bennet croons from the record player in the corner where Aldo places the needle on the spinning black vinyl.

"Aldo," Isabella scolds in a hushed tone. "It's too early for the records. Turn that down."

Obediently he lowers the volume, and I am glad that my father is not there to hear the strings of the orchestra or those songs from the old days in our Cannaregio home—one song blending into the next: *I Cover the Waterfront, The Second Time Around, It Had to Be You.* I lie there and listen and looking down I can see my mother whose ears quiver ever so slightly while she keeps stirring with a wooden spoon.

"Aldo."

"Yes, Mama."

"Enough of the Americans. Play *l'Orfeo*."

Aldo replaces Tony Bennet on the turntable with the music of Monteverdi—not Venetian by birth but who later in life embraced our city as his own. The shed now reverberates with the bright and brassy prologue, its trumpet, trombone and drum—with Aldo climbing onto a stool to conduct the unseen orchestra with twitching paws and an earnest expression that makes me smile.

Giuseppe pushes aside the curtain that separates his bedding from the kitchen. He crosses the earthen floor toward Isabella and nudges her affectionately under the ear before sitting down at the makeshift table, a pine plank set on cinderblocks. He is joined by Aldo who sits beside him while into each bowl Isabella ladles a scoop of polenta. The young maestro plunges his muzzle into the bowl and gobbles his breakfast noisily.

With his head slightly cocked as he chews, Giuseppe though speechless deeply attends to the aria now playing. It is sung by the spirit of music in which she promises to "calm every troubled heart." Watching him, I see why the workers of Venice first flocked to the opera houses of Venice and how for us this music has always spoken to our souls.

Giuseppe rises, then licking Isabella goodbye and followed by Aldo, he steps out onto the alley. Outside I hear the sound of metal wheels rumbling along the paving stones. Then tearing back a corner of the newspaper from the window, I see the rubbish collector approach, pushing the silver cart in which he places the neatly bagged garbage that has been set outside the doorsteps, hanging from hooks beyond the reach of rodents, stray dogs and hungry cats.

As a pup I would sometimes follow a cart to the edge of the canal. There I would watch the crane of the green city barge reach out to grasp and raise the cart as the bottom dropped open and the garbage tumbled down into its hold. I used to wonder where the barge took all that trash with its smells both foul and appetizing. When one day Papa explained how it was taken and turned into pellets that created the electricity for our city, I did not fully understand but thought it a marvelous transformation.

From the loft I watch Giuseppe put on his canvas gloves and take a broom from the cart before lumbering down the narrow street, turning the corner toward the canal. I cannot help but smile to see young Aldo running to keep up with the older males, much as I used to chase after Alfonso wherever he went.

I climb down the ladder to where my mother sets down a crusty loaf of bread, a cup of apricot jam alongside a plate with rough cuts of cheese. Before I can take my seat, I am surrounded by the pups who have leapt up fully awake and are begging at the table. "Zio, Zio, Zio," they yip as I pull off bits of bread to toss to them.

"That's for Piccolo," Mama scolds. "Now go lie down!"

But of course, they do not, continuing to devour the chunks of provolone that they catch mid-air.

"Don't, Piccolo, you'll spoil them."

Which in fact she already has, much as she had done me—not by the number of things she gave but by the abundance of her loving attention. But when I was growing up, she had lavished it on one pup instead of four—perhaps contributing to my youthful at times naïve nature which only in recent months has been jolted into manhood.

"Where is your father? Tell him his breakfast is ready."

"He's gone," I say and see the shadow pass over her face—the shadow that first appeared that day in her studio when Papa had announced his plan to leave for America. But as quickly as it crosses her brow, she puts on the mask with the same false smile as the ones that hang in the souvenir shops of Venice.

"Well then, you will just have to bring it to him."

While she packs a bag with cheese and bread, I move toward the duffel bag in the corner. Having no use for a grinder or torch or any tool of my trade in the foreseeable future, I leave them in the bag slumped against the wall and take only the blue drawstring purse that holds the wallet still fat with Mason's kitchen money. I slip it over my shoulder and move toward the door. The pups nipping at my paws, I gently kick them back inside the shed while leaning in to lick Isabella, who grabs hold of my muzzle and kisses my brow.

"Son, come back to us tonight."

But this is a promise I cannot make because I know wherever my father sleeps, I will be there with him. And in that pause, she nods and half smiles in a way that tells me that she knows that neither Papa nor I will be returning. The door creaks behind me, and I step out onto the paving stones where rain forms tiny rivulets between them.

How flat and pale my city looks to me now, drained of the promises of youth with nothing to fill that void—no youthful enthusiasm, no passion for art, no belief in the possibilities of the future. Even when an attractive female says good morning, I look away. Just yesterday I would have taken a moment to chat or at least admired her curves from behind as she departed. It is as if my brain has been disconnected—the smells that used to trigger hunger, joy, desire and a hundred ideas for new artworks now depress me and only deepen my self-loathing, a disgust that intensifies as I approach la Mola where an old dog in a pork pie hat stares out blankly at the water.

I sit down on the bench beside him and wait for the day to pass.

He does not speak.

The next day I sit by his side and the day after that. When a passerby leaves a half-eaten sandwich on a sheet of wax paper, I grumble at the misconception that we are like beggars by a bridge. But then I realize that is the low point to which we are sinking fast. After our second day on the bench, I feel a hand forcefully shaking me awake. Eye-level with a police officer's white holster, I remain quiet despite a burning sensation in my chest. I sit up surprised to see a female with a mass of black curls tumbling from beneath her white cap with the shiny black visor.

"Are you alright?" she asks with a kindness that cools my anger.

"I'm fine," I reply looking up into her hazel eyes. "But my father he is not well."

We have a brief conversation, and when she asks if I have heard the siren alerting of the oncoming acqua alta, I thank her for her concern. But when she mentions the animal shelter on Lido, she might as well have spat at me. I look away and tell her that we do indeed have a home—but as she walks away, I feel ashamed of the lie and know that I must come up with a plan to avert any further humiliation.

Barely conscious of himself and much less of me, my father slumps deeper and deep into depression. Being a young dog, I know I can withstand the rigors of living outdoors but having lived twelve years Papa is already old. And I know his health has been compromised by the brutality of his imprisonment in that cellar and sleeping on the cold ground.

And so, with the blue drawstring bag slung over my shoulder, I go in search of a realtor who can rent us a room. I head toward Cannaregio, the district that had always been home, but knowing that the water will rise more quickly in the Piazza where I must leave my father, I know I have to hurry.

Taking the backstreets and alleys of San Marco, I zigzag between locals and tourists, some laughing and some cursing as I run between them, slowing only to cross the Rio de Apostoli where a bunch of tourists clog the bridge. I turn onto the Strada Nova where I enter the first realtor's office I pass. Pushing open the screen door, I see two women, identical in all but their blouses seated at the same desk.

"How can we help you?" the realtors ask in unison. Not sure which one to address, I speak to the space between them and say that I am looking for a rental.

The one on the left in the green shirt asks if I am in town for the *Regatta Storica*, the annual boat races that have been held in

Venice for over 500 years.

"What? Do I look like a tourist?"

She apologizes, explaining that she detects an American accent, a compliment that diminishes my irritation.

"Thanks."

Turning her attention to the screen of her device, she tells me that given the time of year, she might be able to locate something for 2000 a month. I try not to show my surprise and quickly invent a story that my father and I are waiting for repairs to be completed on our condo in San Marco, so that we only need a room for a week.

We are in luck. She mentions that a friend's niece has to travel out of town and has just dropped off her keys a few minutes ago for them to sublet her studio in Cannaregio.

"How much?"

The sister on the right wearing a crisp yellow blouse explains she wants 450 for the week, but that if I pay cash, I can have it for 400 plus 15% finder's fee.

"How much in dollars?"

As quickly as green shirt takes a calculator from her top drawer, yellow shirt responds. "At the current exchange rate, three hundred seventy."

Green shirt glances up and smiles, "My sister has always been good with numbers."

I count out the American dollars then fold the thin wallet and replace it in the drawstring bag. In unison they ask me to take a seat and fill out the application. Then the one in yellow calls the apartment owner to ask if she will consider renting to my kind.

"My kind? My kind has built and adorned this city." I grumble, but neither female is listening. The one in green is now chatting with a couple who have entered with a stroller while her sister is tapping on her device. She looks up and asks how many of us will be occupying the place.

"Only my father and I."

Yellow blouse puts down the phone, takes my application and reaches into her drawer for a key on a large ring. She takes a business card from the holder and jots down the owner's name and number. "If there's a problem, don't call us, call Anna. It's on the *Fondamente Nove*."

She clasps the card between her black lacquered nails and passes it to me. "Far from the tourists, and you can take a boat to Murano."

"Or to San Michele to visit the dead," her sister chimes in with a laugh.

"Cemeteries don't interest me," I reply put off by the strange joke.

"And no females!"

I laugh to myself—no females? For if I am fortunate enough to find a female willing to visit, she will indeed be welcome. Leaving the office, I feel anxious that I have spent most of our money but proud to hold the key to my first apartment.

I hurry to San Marco where the water has already flooded the Piazza and the walkways have been set up by the city workers. As I swim to the place where I left Papa, I see his pork pie hat, bobbing toward me like a little boat. I snatch it in my teeth and jump onto the bench beside him where the tide has risen above his paws and covers his muzzle. He gasps and coughs as I shake him roughly.

"Why, Papa? Why?"

He stands beside me, dripping and forlorn. "Why live?"

"And me? I am nothing? And what of all you taught me, all that fine talk? Now you spit in the face of life and roll over, begging death to buckle its collar around your neck and snap on its leash?"

Papa sneezes loudly.

"To honor life is to honor pain."

"Yes, my son, you are right."

"Now come. I rented a place in Cannaregio. Follow me." We

swim toward the Basilica where tourists looking down from the walkways crazily click our picture. Toward our neighborhood the waters recede, and we splash across courtyards where after several wrong turns, we arrive at the doorway of the house that will briefly be our home. I worry that our sublet might be on the first floor still blurry under a centimeter of water when a young man enters in waist high boots.

"You guys lost?"

I am stung by the assumption that our kind might not also be tenants. "We are subletting from Anna. Do you know what floor she's on?"

The stranger is a barrel-chested guy with a full beard who wears a shirt of plaid with the sleeves rolled up, revealing on one muscular forearm a foaming wave—an image copied from Hokusai, the Japanese painter of the Edo period whose work so influenced my mother's watercolors.

"Nice tattoo."

"Thanks, I'm Francesco Carante."

"And I am Piccolo Fortunato, and this my father, Alfonso."

Francesco nods toward Papa who is panting. "Is he okay?"

"He's had a long day."

"Let me give you a hand." He lifts my father and carries him up the marble slabs. We stop on the third landing where I fumble with the key until the tumbler turns. And when I push open the green door, a cathedral could not have looked grander. A pale blue light through the windows falls like a bedsheet over the sparsely furnished living room. After Francesco gently sets Papa down on the futon, I follow him to the door where he steps into the corridor.

"Just give me a shout if you guys need anything."

"We'll be okay, thanks."

I shut the door and cross to the bathroom, taking a thick white towel that smells of bleach and lavender from behind the frosted glass door of the cabinet to rub down my father who is now shivering. I dry him off and help him back onto the couch where I pull a quilt over him before heading into the galley kitchen where in the cabinet I find a tin of Lavazza and one of biscotti. Though it takes me a minute to figure out Anna's espresso machine, I make us some coffee and join Papa in the living room. Side by side we eat our snack and care nothing about the rain splattering against the glass panel of the door that leads to the balcony overlooking the lagoon and in the hazy distance Isola San Michele—the island that the brief conqueror Napoleon designated for the dead of Venice, but where some claim there is more life than is suspected. However, having been raised by my father to be a rational thinker, I dismiss such superstitions.

For the next two days Papa rests. Budgeting our remaining dollars to afford food for several weeks, I buy some beef from the butcher who throws in some marrow bones. The beef we eat raw, but the next day I boil the bones with the garlic and shallots that I find in a basket under the counter to make an incredible soup, enhanced by the pleasure of gnawing the gristle off the bone.

On the third day of our rental, my father goes on the balcony and looks out at the lagoon.

"The day is approaching, Piccolo. Soon it will be here."

I step out onto the narrow terrace and inhale deeply. I smell a passing garbage barge, I smell a nest of newborn rats, I smell the pistachio torte—ah the pistachio torte, fresh from the oven of the pasticceria down the street, but I cannot detect who or what my father is awaiting with such anticipation.

And then I catch a whiff of her—earthy and clean as the air after a light rain. She must have smelt me also because she looks up, her black eyes sending a shiver through me.

"Ciao, bella," I call down to her. "What is your name?"

Perhaps she thinks me too familiar, or that her name is too great a gift to give, but her sleek body retreats into the apartment below although I do detect the slightest wag.

But who is this mysterious neighbor? And how might I see her again? I consider going downstairs and knocking boldly on her door but given the cold response I just received, I decide to wait until we meet by chance on the stairs or in the vestibule. I am rehearsing the lines that I might say to her at that fortunate moment when my father scratches on the green door.

"Come, Piccolo, we must wait at the Piazzetta."

The streets are now dry, and my father is feeling strong. We walk along the Canalasso from our district to San Marco, heading toward the busy promenade when through the crowd emerges an angry Isabella who scolds us loudly for having disappeared. She moans and groans about how worried she has been before smacking my muzzle lightly and then kissing my head.

"I'm sorry, Mama, but Papa needed a dry place and so I rented us a place in Cannaregio."

"You have always been a clever pup." With a half-smile, she takes out a napkin and pen from her basket in which on this rare occasion all four pups are napping, squeaking and twitching in their sleep.

"Write down where you are staying."

As I do so, she removes the plastic lid from a container of *risi i bisi* still warm from the pot. My father tells her that we are not hungry, but she leaves the tasty rice studded with green peas on the bench and by noon the container is empty.

Each evening we return to our rooms, and each morning we return to the quay looking out on the Basino di San Marco where we continue to wait—but Papa will still not say why. On the sixth day of our rental, my father's eyes are wide with anticipation. When we leave Anna's place to head for our usual bench, he takes her *carello* from the hall closet.

"Why the cart?"

"Because something tells me that today is the day to prepare for the arrival."

As I follow my father, pulling the cart behind me along the paving stones, I mutter to myself and wonder when my time will come to be on my own. As we pass a small wineshop not far from the Ponce di Rialto, Papa enters, then without consulting me, spends the last of our money on a case of Prosecco and a package of small plastic cups. At the quay, he takes one of the bottles from the cart, pops it open and before he drinks, he offers it to me. "Go ahead, take a whiff."

I take in its vibrant, fruity bouquet but would much rather taste than sniff.

"Go ahead, drink."

"Ah, yes," I say after a long swig. "Apple, peach and some sort of wildflower."

"Very good, son, and honeysuckle." He drinks deeply. "Ah, the honeysuckle." And when Isabella returns, she does not find Alfonso moping on the bench, but chasing pigeons in the Piazzetta revivified by the sparkling wine.

He runs to her wagging his tail, bouncing playfully around her. She pauses taken aback by this sudden rush of good feeling, reminiscent of how my father used to be when we were a young and happy family. She sneezes repeatedly when my father climbs onto the bench, stands and places his hat over his heart, reaching out his other paw toward her. And as he sings to her, he does indeed look bewitched, bothered and bewildered.

Their eyes lock. In a trance Isabella puts down the basket of sleeping puppies while he serenades her, complaining in the words of the old Gershwin tune, that he could not sleep and would not sleep, how in fact love told him that he should not sleep.

Among the passersby who gather on the promenade, a musician with his bow tie dangling from his collar on his way home from a gig, stops to listen. He snaps open the case and takes out a small trumpet to accompany the old Italian greyhound in the battered hat who sings from the bench with his whole body—his ears, his paws, his tail all moving with emotion that moves the crowd.

But Alfonso is not singing for them, he is singing only to her, longing for the day when he will cling to her—the silvery notes of the trumpet dancing with his voice, swirling above our heads and toward the sea. Then Alfonso's voice slides into another song, charming Isabella with one of their old favorites by Ray Noble—the songwriter whose name I recall because my father so often quizzed me on composers when I was a pup. Isabella smiles as he sings of when he thinks of her, how he forgets to do the ordinary things that canines ought to do. And when he sings of his longing, he taps his chest, and in response she taps her own.

Standing at the hub of that admiring audience, bobbing, swaying, some singing along off key, only I can see the agony that eddies below the bars of the music like unseen, murky currents beneath a pier—while rising above us, each lithe note convinces all who have gathered for a moment of the joy of life. Even my mother stands radiant in that intoxicating belief, drawing closer to the singer, unaware of the puppies who are slipping out of the basket to run wild along the quay. Only Aldo stays by her side, entranced by the songs that he has heard over and over on the old record player in the corner of the shed—scratchy echoes that now come to life in the open air when sung by a lover to his beloved.

And then as his voice wavers on the last note, he steps from the bench and places his pork pie hat on his head before stretching out his paws toward his funny valentine—his sweet and funny valentine whose laughable looks, in the words of Richard Rogers, are unphotographable. And he nods toward the fawn color greyhound who he claims as his favorite work of art.

Standing on the bench, he tilts his head and implores her with his eyes to dance. And so, Isabella enters his open arms as easily as she would walk into her own bedroom. Then in the space the crowd creates for the twirling couple, Isabella holds her short-legged husband close to her breast as he sings the song with which he, a penniless sculptor, had wooed her, a penniless beauty, by the Rialto Bridge.

And for a moment the singing stops as Alfonso laughs to himself when he comes to that line in the song when he asks his funny valentine—are you smart? I laugh too at the little inside joke because we both know that Isabella, beyond smart is a genius at life and loving.

Then I catch the scent of another musician who approaches, citrusy and bright, wheeling along her instrument. She has short-cropped hair and wears a long black skirt that billows in the breeze, and catching sight of my admiring gaze, she gives me a little wave to which I respond with a little wag. Then unsnapping her case, she takes out her cello and sets its endpin on the stones and begins sliding her bow over the strings as my parents spin and dip the way they used to in our Cannaregio home. And when my father comes to the last line of the song, begging his funny valentine to stay, in the distance three puppies yap. And at that moment, my mother shakes off the charm that has bewitched her and runs, seemingly in search of her three babies, but in reality to break the spell my father has cast with the American songs that had been their own.

And watching her sleek figure flee—the love of his life who for a moment he had beguiled—he stands alone. His voice diminishes to barely a whisper. But when he comes to the final line, Aldo parts his jaws and from his narrow chest arise the most remarkable notes. The crowd is amazed by the singing puppy whose voice carries the last syllables that are shimmering in the air—Val…en…tine's day.

It is then Alfonso collapses under the lethargy from which he had so briefly escaped. Only I am aware of this as tourists and locals alike applaud and throw money from around the world at the old dog who lies motionless while beside him stands the pup, shocked at the sudden emergence of his own voice and at the excitement of the crowd.

"Encore, encore," they shout.

The cellist leans over to Aldo and asks if he knows any other songs.

"Only from the one about Orfeo. That's my mother's favorite

opera."

"Which one? Gluck or Monteverdi?"

"She likes Monteverdi."

And so, after a moment's conference with the other musicians who have joined us, the Piazzetta is transformed into the underworld as Aldo sings, *Torna O Bella.* I am struck by the irony of his choice, the farewell of the blessed spirits that arrive at the end of the second act when Orfeo and Eurydice begin their ill-fated journey from Hades back to earth.

On the edge of the crowd, Isabella reappears, chasing the pups back to the basket when she sees that it is her own son who has mesmerized the crowd. As the last crystal note dissolves in the warm air, all stand in silence—except the three pups who run about wildly collecting the bills and coins that the audience, released from its trance, continue to toss toward the bench.

"Keep singing, keep singing," the puppies yap. But sensing the pain of the old singer, Aldo lies down beside him. Neither moves.

Then Isabella approaches and bends to take Aldo in her arms when suddenly Alfonso lifts his head and kisses her. Startled, she stares deeply into the eyes of the only dog she has ever truly loved.

"Alfonso," she begins.

But before she can speak what is in her heart, Alfonso sits up alert—his nose twitching, his ears pinned back.

"She's here."

And without a backward glance, he runs along the edge of the canal to where a blue UPS barge approaches, piled high with boxes that surround a tall crate. Alfonso wags his tail furiously and barks for me to join him.

"Papa, what?"

"Iona, Iona has arrived!" he shouts to the crowd. "Our sculpture from New York! Come and see our greatest work of art!"

It is then watching my mother gather up her pups to place in the basket and run back to her home in Giuseppe's shed, I realize that all these years, despite Alfonso's proclamations of love, he openly has kept a mistress. She is the same mistress who drew him to New York City, the same mistress who mistreated and robbed him of two years in that rat-infested cellar, the same mistress who having followed him home to Venice, now is calling him away from his wife. Sculpture has always been and would always be his first love, no matter how big the price he would pay or the amount of pain he would inflict on my mother—an obsession that I now understand undermined their marriage and ironically his career as irreversibly as the waters of the lagoon are slowly washing Venice away.

"Iona, Iona," he barks as the crane of the barge lifts the crate and sets it on the quay. I watch my father speak with the worker and sign the clipboard, accepting the package that was sent to us from our good friend, Mason Maldonado.

"A hammer," he cries out leaping from the barge. "Does anyone have a hammer?"

A workman stops as curious as the other passers-by who have gathered and setting down his toolbox removes a small crowbar that he hands to the excited dog. "Yes, this will do," says my father as he begins to pry off the slats of the crate.

"Piccolo, get the cups and the Prosecco!"

No longer enamored of art, I feel duped by its idolatry of things that eclipse our real valuables—the relationships with those who are foolish enough to love us. In no mood to celebrate, I return to the bench to fetch the cart with the eleven remaining bottles of wine. Aldo walks beside me.

"Brother, what's in the big box?"

"Just a sculpture."

"What's a sculpture.?"

"Just a thing."

"Is it beautiful?"

"Not nearly as beautiful as you, Aldo, or our mother."

We walk back toward the barge where my father stands on the

quay beside Iona whose voluptuous form we sanded and rubbed with tung oil back in Brooklyn so that now in the light off the lagoon, her grain shines with new luster.

"Wine for everyone," my father shouts.

And so, I lift Aldo and wrap my left arm around his freckled belly. And while he holds out the stack of cups for each guest at our impromptu art reception to grab one, I serve the Prosecco. Alfonso now raises his own plastic cup.

"My friends, and I call you my friends because here in Venice we natives and newcomers are bound by the ancient felicity of this city. Today I present to you, Iona, the island dove, a Venetian beauty who has returned home. Yes, she was carved of wood grown in America, but that does not make her American." He pauses and surveys the crowd with a serious look and then smiles. "Because like Botticelli's Venus, Iona was born of an Italian dream by an Italian dreamer who today sets free the spirit of Iona here in her homeland to dwell for all time among the Madonnas of Venice."

Papa raises his cup as do all the people in the crowd. "Long live Iona!"

"Long live Iona," they chant in response.

"And in our joy, let us not forget all those who are caged—some by steel, others by lies. Shackled by their keepers—lust and greed. Like them I too was chained to the ego of a man whose demented will I was forced to serve. How did I survive? In my heart I remained free, knowing that freedom will always prevail—for no male, no female, no offspring was born to be the property of another." Papa raises his cup and cries, "Freedom for all!!

"Freedom for all!"

The trumpeter now raises his horn and plays four notes as the crowd continues to chant, "Freedom for all!"

"Freedom for all," I sing out with Aldo from the edge of the crowd.

Then glancing at his watch, the trumpeter returns his

instrument to its case, doffs his cap and hurries down the quay just as two violinists—either on their way to a gig or coming home from one—join the cellist. They whisper with Papa, selecting the next piece. And then beautifully they recreate spring as composed by Vivaldi.

From their strings rise crosscurrents of breezes that drive off winter, and in this concerto, I hear the patter of rain on the paving stones and the rush of wings of pigeons taking flight as chased by a barking dog. I can imagine the composer, our own Vivaldi, sitting here on the Mola and listening to the music of Venice in the air before returning to his room to jot down its notes.

And so, the day continues with various musicians stopping by, playing a set then heading off as other musicians are drawn into our circle to play and then depart. Some play pop, some jazz and one up-an-coming rapper from L.A. takes the opportunity to sell his CD.

Towards dusk Aldo falls asleep, so I place him in the Prosecco box in the cart where he naps as the crowd begins to disperse. A silver haired couple asks my father where they can find Harry's Bar and are surprised to learn they are only a short walk away along Riva degli Schiavoni. Papa offers to take them there, and with my little brother gently snoring in the cart, we walk the along the promenade to be sure the old ones don't get lost. As the sun sets, they explain that over fifty years ago on their spring break from college, they met there at the bar while ordering Bellinis, and now on their fiftieth anniversary they have returned to order another.

"Fifty years," I murmur.

"Yes, it's a long time to be married," says the woman.

"It's a long time to be alive," I reply, wondering if any of their species appreciates the length of their lifespan.

"Yes, it has been wonderful." She smiles at her husband who with one hand firmly on his cane, reaches out with the other, pulling her close to kiss her hard on the lips. Yes, I think with a pang of envy, some of them do.

Suddenly the male asks if we would join them for the evening.

"Yes, do," says his wife whose name is Melinda. "Jack and I would love that."

So of course, we agree, and we turn down the alley toward Harry's Bar. Passing through the double doors of old wood and frosted glass, we release the currents of conversations and the clatter of silver knives and forks that echo off the walls of the small room, rimmed with a warm amber light. Aldo awakes and peeks out of the cart, and never having been anywhere beyond his father's shed or the few shops he frequents with his mother, he is amazed. Jack sets his claw-foot cane on the floor beside our table and orders four Bellinis and a ginger ale for Aldo who now sits on my lap marveling at the scene, especially the drinks—his being served in a long-stemmed glass, topped with a long-stemmed cherry. Although the bubbles make him sneeze, he laps up the drink and gobbles the cherry, spitting the pit onto the table.

I wipe it up with a napkin. "No, Aldo!"

"Don't scold," says Melinda. "He's just a baby."

Aldo pops up from his seat. "I am not a baby. I am weaned!"

She and her husband laugh heartily which only angers Aldo more. But as I rub his belly and scratch behind his ear, he soon calms down and dozes back to sleep, allowing me to savor my Bellini—mildly sweet and fizzy, the blended flavor of peach with a dash of raspberry tickles my tongue while the alcohol intermingles with the several glasses of Prosecco I drank during the day, making me more than a little light-headed.

When Jack asks to see he menu, my father suggests that he take them back to Cannaregio where we can dine on seafood caught today in the lagoon for a quarter of the price.

Eagerly, the couple agrees, and we set off for our district and a restaurant where my father used to on occasion sing. I worry about Jack who limps along with his cane on what seems to be a shorter leg—but lured by the promise of a good local meal, he and

Melinda walk at a brisk pace, asking questions about our neighborhood, the churches and markets, about our work and our travels. Papa only makes a brief reference to our time in Brooklyn but boasts about my sculpture having been exhibited at the Gallstone Gallery. Melinda is curious about the sculpture on the Canal and is impressed to hear that it was exhibited at the Gauntley Biennial, an event she has never heard of but that she thinks must be very nice.

"Yes, and we got an excellent write up in the review by Martin Kibbleman," my father adds.

"Kibbleman?"

"He writes for the New York Times."

"Oh, yes, I have heard of that."

By the time we arrive at the restaurant, the few outdoor tables that overlook the canal from beneath the overhanging vines are taken, so we enter the dining room where the warm wood, cool light and intermingling smells from the kitchen welcome us. We are seated by Roberto the host, an old friend of Alfonso. Jack asks Papa to order who does so with enthusiasm but cannot help but salivate as he describes each dish while we await our meal.

The seafood antipasti soon arrives—sardines, calamari and a white bowl of blue-black mussels. For a moment I am transported back to another meal and the musky smelling beauty who served it, and I sigh, thinking of how much more Iona means to me than the sculpture on the quay.

"Are you alright?" I hear a distant voice ask.

"Yes," I mutter but then realize that Jack is speaking to his wife who is staring sullenly at the platter. She explains that she has never seen seafood so recently plucked from the sea and served without breading, fries and ketchup. The muscles around her lips tighten and make her for the first time appear old, but with one bite her expression softens, and her eyes express pleasure.

Then come the first platters—the gnocchi with salmon sauce, the tagliolini with lobster and the ravioli. As Melinda and Jack marvel at the food, better than they have ever tasted, Papa pushes aside his plate and shakes his head.

"What's the matter, Alfonso? I thought y'all loved this here seafood?"

Papa assures her it is not the food and excuses himself from the table, stepping outside to get some fresh air. I am about to follow him, but he insists. "No, Piccolo, you stay. Enjoy the meal and the company of our friends."

Never have I seen Papa step away from the table, certainly not without having made a speech. But I do know that the events of this week have been both exhilarating and exhausting, and with the arrival of the squid and polenta, my attention is drawn back to our meal, the pleasure of which is enhanced by the arrival of a musician who plays a Spanish guitar.

In between courses Roberto, a consummate dancer, comes to our table and with Jack's permission, takes Melinda's hand and holds her waist as he places his face to hers and leads her through the steps of a tango. Blushing, Melinda looks like a girl, and Jack watches her with an admiration as if seeing her for the first time.

Hearing that our friends are celebrating their anniversary, Roberto brings to our table four plates of tiramisu—Aldo who has been sleeping on my lap throughout the meal, awakes, his eyes peering over the plate at that spongy block of yellow cake and sweet mascarpone cheese. Careful to scrape the chocolate shavings from its top layer, I feed him his share of that amazing desert—invented in Venice despite what others in Tuscany might claim.

While he seats a couple at a nearby table, Roberto glances over to see Aldo jump up and with four paws on the table devour my dessert. But as I scold the unruly pup who is licking the last smudge from my plate, Roberto brings me a second serving that I much enjoy with my ristretto, the shot of espresso we all agree we need to fuel our way home. Outside Papa awaits us by the canal. He appears very distracted, and we all respect his silence as he trots along by our side.

Because Jack and Melinda must leave Venice early the next morning, we make our way to the pier and wait for the vaporetto to take them back to their hotel in Dorsoduro. Much wine has accompanied each course of our meal, so they are merrily tipsy, but in a city without cars and little crime, I do not worry about our friends who wave from the boat—Melinda blowing kisses and shouting in that distinctly American twang, "Make sure y'all visit us in Texas!"

Aldo, who along with his stolen tiramisu also lapped up a few sips of wine, falls back to sleep in his box. I consider wheeling him home to his mother, but it is late, and I know Giuseppe rises early, so I decide against it, reassuring myself that having our address, Isabella has no need to worry about her pup.

While we walk down the Rio Terà della Maddelena toward the building that will be home for one more night, I brush aside the worry of where we will live next. As we cross the courtyard, I notice Papa's legs are wobbly for a couple of steps, and then he stumbles, stopping to sit at the base of the stone cistern.

"Papa, are you alright?"

"Yes," he growls somewhat irritably. "You go ahead."

Of course, I wait until he rises and steadies himself and we cross the courtyard toward the building. In the vestibule I lift Aldo from the cart to carry him upstairs when I notice that Papa's hind legs are slipping on the marble floor beneath him. When I move toward him to assist, he waves me away then tries with his powerful chest and forelegs to pull himself onto the bottom step. Fortunately, Francesco enters whistling happily with his arm around a pretty female who whistles along with him. But when he sees Papa struggling with one leg folded beneath him and the other splayed outward to the right, he goes to him.

"I'm alright," Papa snarls.

"I know, my friend, but we can all use a hand once in a while, right?" Francesco kneels and positions his arms like a forklift beneath Papa to carry him upstairs. I can sense Papa's shame and the sadness of the pretty woman who follows silently behind us.

"Piccolo," says Francesco over his shoulder. "This is Anna."

"Anna?" I blurt out. "But you are not supposed to be back until tomorrow."

"Yes, I got home early, but no worries. I'll stay with Francesco. The place is yours for the night."

"Thank you," I reply feeling a pang of envy, for as much as I like Francesco and wish him well in all things including love, I deeply desire the warmth of a female beside me through the night, the necking and the nuzzling, the conversations and whatever else might follow. I sigh as we continue up the stairs.

At the green door I fumble with the key, this time because the lovely Anna is standing so close, and I find her blend of perspiration and haircare products overwhelming. Her soft, moist hand covers my paw as she turns the key and then leads us to her bed where she pulls back the goose down comforter. Francesco lays my papa down on the white cotton sheets. He then leans over and puts his head to my father's chest from which comes a rattling breath like shallow water over stones.

"How old is he?" Anna asks in a low voice.

"Papa is almost twelve. But he's had hard times, and the last two have been like ten."

"Stay with him, Piccolo. I have to leave for work early, so I'll check on you in the morning."

"Thanks, Francesco," I say to the man who a week ago had been a stranger but who has become a deeply trusted friend. I walk them to the door where I lick his hand, and he scratches me behind the ear.

After Francesco and Anna leave, Aldo climbs down from the futon where I left him and follows me into the bedroom and looks up at the bed. He nods for me to lift him to lie beside Alfonso on whose chest he rests his head. I pull over a wicker chair and sit by my father's bedside, holding his calloused paw between my own. His eyes open and seem to focus on a distant point, and his breathing becomes more labored.

"Piccolo," he says, his voice raspy.

"I'm here, Papa."

"Piccolo, help me."

"Yes, Papa."

"Help me… get… back home."

"Yes, Papa."

For a moment, I think he is delirious, for we are no longer on the street and any home he ever had, he left it long ago. But then something within me says that this night has been appointed for Alfonso to make a longer journey, the journey that all living things must make when we shed our mortality to become the stuff of planets and stars—a journey on which my father is asking me to accompany him, and so closing my eyes, I let intuition lead the way.

Moving in reverse, my mind takes us back to the restaurant, only this time Alfonso savors each dish until a vacuum through the open door pulls us from the table and out onto the street—sucking us back to the promenade where all the music of that day replays, a pleasant cacophony in my mind. There as the water of the Canal splashes over the edge of the quay, Roberto dances with a blushing American wife. And there they are joined, spinning and swaying, grasping and gliding, by all the strangers who had stopped to celebrate with us that day, along with all our friends and enemies from recent years, including the spirit of Guy Gizàrd who waltzes with a much younger Mason Maldonado.

Then the cellist with short hair twirls before me, her long black skirt fluttering in the mist, reaching out for me to dance. But before I can place my forelegs around her slender waist, a warm wind blows off the lagoon and sweeps us from the square and down the Strada Nuovo, past the shops and over the heads of the tourists until we land back in our old place in Cannaregio. There from her studio, Isabella watches with sadness as Alfonso reaches for his pork pie hat—but pauses to replace it on the nail and turn to her to say, "I'll stay."

Now the three of us cross the living room to sit on the low sofa where Isabella's beauty is amplified in the low light cast by the shaded lamp. Feeling contentment, I start to doze off when through my partially closed eyes, I watch Alfonso and Isabella nuzzle and lick.

A knock at the door rouses me from my reverie. I know before I open it that Isabella has arrived. We exchange no words for she already knows and rushes to Alfonso's bedside. She kisses his head and strokes his brow.

With much effort, my father speaks, and his words emerge, half-concealed beneath his raspy breaths.

"You... have... all... been so... wonderful."

Aldo inches closer to the singer's face and licks gently as does my mother. I hold his paw more firmly, half-believing I can hold him there with us if only for a little while longer.

But in his chest I hear the gurgle like the waters of the acqua alta rising, and then his eyes still open, his spirit departs.

My mother blesses herself and rocks silently, comforting Aldo who has crawled onto her lap while I sit, holding his paw unwilling to let go—like sitting on a boulder still warm from the day's heat as the sun begins to set. And then as the stone grows cold, you know you must get up to go for soon it will be dark.

But still you sit.

Just as the dawn filters through the curtain, a knock at the door brings us back from the realm where we have spent the night with my father's spirit, hovering above the mundane reality of beds and bureaus and worldly concerns. So, when Francesco and Anna enter, bringing us back to this world without Alfonso, my mother howls like a wind trapped in a courtyard, stirring up the leaves and rising in a fury toward the rooftops.

Encircling her long slim arms around Isabella and Aldo, Anna leads them from the bedroom to the kitchen while Francesco wraps my father in the comforter and carries him downstairs. I follow him onto the street and walk beside him to the office of the local vet whose clinic is not yet open, but who comes downstairs when I ring the bell.

The doctor leads us through the backdoor and down a long corridor with peeling yellow wallpaper into a dim office where he tells Francesco to leave the body on the steel table. He has witnessed this family scene many times before, knowing that while most choose to leave the bodies of the departed of our kind to be picked up in a bag left on the street like so much rubbish, others choose to give their loved ones a more respectful end. Francesco pays the doctor who asks if we want the ashes.

"No," I reply.

While still with the spirit of my father throughout the night, I was calm, balanced in the knowledge he had given me that death is no more than pushing open the glass door of the cinema and stepping out into the night. And it was in that netherworld that we had remained together—until entering this office, assaulted by the truncheon smells of antiseptic and urine reeking of fear, I return to my senses, only to realize that he is no longer in his. And realize that with him, something within me has died.

And as Francesco speaks quietly with the vet, I break down. I choke on my own breath, heaving. I pull back the blanket in which he is wrapped, and my drool moistens the mass of dry fur and bones that had been my father. Francesco and the kind doctor try to console me until his assistant leads in a small nervous dog on a leash.

"Come, Piccolo." Francesco leads me out of the office and down the alley, my head bent toward the pavers—the stones that now are only stone, that used to seem so alive to me, echoing with a thousand years of footfalls and the padding of paws. Where I used to hear the hum of history, there is now only silence.

It is a strange sensation as if the serrated blade of a bread knife has cut my soul from me. I note a boy and a dog passing by on two ends of a leash, two males with their arms locked at the elbow, a female with a big-headed baby looking out wide-eyed from its pouch and realize that I am alone. Unlike those creatures, I am severed from my friend and father. And that I am a solitary dog in the world.

I recall how as a pup looking up through the bars of our balcony at the flittering cosmos, I wondered how many stars it contained. And my mother who sat beside me said that it was an ever-changing number as stars like us are born and die each day.

"Stars die?"

"Hundreds of millions each day."

Still my mind cannot grasp so large a number, but now I know having witnessed the snuffing out of a single star in the night that the cosmos must be a sad and ever-grieving place.

All this passes as in a dream, even now an old dog looking back on those days, I wonder how I made it back to Anna's place as every impulse drew me toward the edge of the Canalasso to dive into those murky waters and swim until I could swim no more, to be or cease to be in the place where my father did or did not dwell.

5 On My Own

The weathered door of Anna's building seems to weep, the rivulets of rain running down its surface, chafed and pitted as the skin of an old man's face. Francesco turns the key and holds the door open for me.

"I'm sorry I have to work today."

"I understand."

"Where will you be living now that Anna is back? Do you need a place to stay?"

"I am not homeless." I immediately regret my Fortunato pride.

"Sorry, man." Francesco holds my muzzle between his thick hands and bends to kiss my brow. "Let me know if you need anything." I stare at the stone slab beneath my paws. "Anything."

Francesco kneels, and we embrace. His warmth reminds me that I am very cold and as he hurries off, I turn to climb the stairs to Anna's place where I find the door ajar. Isabella is sitting on the futon beside Aldo who yaps lightly in his sleep.

Anna enters from the kitchen and sets down two mugs of steaming tea on the mosaic table beside a plate with long slices of semolina bread spread with soft cheese. Aldo's nostrils quiver, then his eyes pop before jumping up on the table to grab a piece of bread.

Listless I stand with my paws by my side until Anna's cool hand leads me to the wicker chair where I sit and stare blankly before me. Beyond the smell of sharp goat cheese, from deep inside the cave of my grief, I smell something oddly familiar—earthy and fresh like a flowering bush in a yard newly fertilized. I turn toward the bedroom where I see her again with her black, soulful eyes peering out from the doorway. She is the same exquisite female I had spied from the balcony. And just as on that first encounter, she retreats as quickly as she senses my gaze.

"That's Chiara. She's very shy."

"I notice she walks with a limp," my mother observes.

"Yes, I found her at a shelter, or what they call a shelter in Naples. She was in a filthy cage where she was sleeping on the bare cement, so now she has joint problems."

"I have heard of those foul places," Isabella replies. "Where men take money from the government to keep the dogs, many still children, in those prisons."

"My editor sent me to do a story, the stench and the sounds of them whimpering were unbearable. I felt so angry that my taxes pay for these horrible places, but what could I do? And then one pup stared up from the cage, and I knew I had to save her. I gave the guy twenty euros so I could put her under my coat and take her home without all the paperwork. That was like two years ago."

"She is as beautiful as a Bellini, but with a sadness even he could not have captured."

"Actually, Piccolo, she is much better than when I first brought her home. But she still tends to keep to herself, and she's so skittish that I have to walk her late at night and very early in the morning before anyone is out."

Just as I am imaging ways to befriend Chiara, to protect her and gain her trust, Anna crushes that seminal hope.

"I'm not sure how she will take to New York."

"New York?"

"Yes, tomorrow. The semester at Columbia starts next week, why?"

"Oh. Nothing."

My mother sets down her steaming white mug on the black tiles of the tabletop. "But Anna, New York City is a terrible place. Why would you leave Italy?"

"For the same reason a lot of my friends have left. Italy has no use for us or our education."

"That is very sad, very sad indeed." My mother shakes her muzzle unaware that Aldo has just nabbed the last slice of bread which he carries off to a corner, his belly bloated, making him look like a small barrel. "Well, I must get home to take care of the babies. Come, Aldo. Come, Piccolo."

So easily my mother has lapsed into the belief that I am still a pup. At first, I had found it oddly amusing and was willing to play along, however, it has become embarrassing, especially now with Chiara within range to hear her.

"Yes, Isabella. Let's take Aldo home."

"Isabella?" Her voice expresses shock and indignation. "Now I'm Isabella?"

"Mama," I say, trying to placate her while glancing toward the bedroom to see if Chiara is in the doorway.

"Hmph." My mother rises from her chair and moves toward the door.

"Hmph," repeats Aldo.

I look to Anna and grin uncomfortably and am glad to find sympathy in her eyes. She tilts her head toward the kitchen for me to follow.

"Listen, I get it. After I graduated from NYU, I couldn't find a job in New York or any company who would sponsor me. So, I had to move back home, sleep in my old room, my old bed, staring at the decorations from my bat mitzvah. I get it. It's humiliating. But trust me, things will change."

I nod although I don't understand NYU or bat mitzvah. But I do understand that Anna is an ally and sees me as a peer which I deeply appreciate. When I hear the sound of nails tapping on the hardwood floor, I turn quickly to see Chiara approaching the kitchen and then turn to retreat into the bedroom.

"And I'm sorry about Chiara. She's just really shy."

"I understand," I say loud enough so that she will hear me. "I understand her hardship and much admire her beauty and her strength."

"Piccolo!" Isabella calls from the corridor.

When Anna leans over to embrace me, it is as if I have stuck my nose into a bush of roses that has been warmed by the sun on a cloudless day. I feel the muscles of her arms slacken, but before she releases me from the hug, I nuzzle her neck with my nose.

"Are you on Facebook?"

"A book of faces."

"Yeah, well kind of. But never mind, no big deal. I'm not on there much myself. Let's stay in touch through Francesco."

"Piccolo, now!"

"Sorry, Isabella. I just wanted to thank Piccolo for taking such good care of my place."

"Yes, he is a very good boy."

Mortified I shake my head and step out into the hall to avoid any further humiliation. But Anna gives me a reassuring wink and before she shuts the door, I catch a final glimpse of Chiara watching our departure, and I carve the image of her well-formed head like a cameo in my mind.

Silently I cross the courtyard that only a day before I had crossed with Alfonso, and with each step I feel the chasm between us widen. We had been reunited for such a short time—staying up late in the piano bar on the ship, laughing, talking, sketching diagrams on napkins of the layout of our new studio and the next series of artwork we would sculpt together. And as I move further from the last place we had shared on earth, I feel myself moving away from those dreams and the passion that used to burn in me to make art now crumble into a mound of smoldering ash.

I follow Isabella who wrapped in the mantilla of her own grief walks in a daze, pushing the cart with Aldo asleep in the Prosecco box in front of her. When we reach Giuseppe's shed, I climb the steps to the loft, lie down and pull the rough blanket over my head. Days shift into evenings and evenings into nights. I stir only to step outside to pee in the alley, take a sip of water from the kitchen faucet before escaping again into a deep sleep—until one afternoon when loud cheers arise over the rooftops, drowned out by a chorus of whining from below.

"Mama, Mama, it's started. The boats, Mama, we want to see the boats."

"No. No boats today." Isabella noisily grates a horseradish, ignoring their pleas and the far-off shouts of the cheering crowd that remind me of an afternoon long ago when I was awoken by my father.

"Come," he had commanded with excitement, reaching for his pork pie. I leapt from the sofa to follow him out the door and down the steps, racing through the back alleys of Cannaregio to the end of Castello where the races had begun. As a pup, I was thrilled to see the big boats ornamented with serpents and rearing silver horses and to hear the splash of the gondoliers' oars.

That had been my first *Regata Storica*, but as we nosed our way to the edge of the crowd, my father told me that these processions down the Canalasso dated back for hundreds of years. Finding a spot to better see the boats and oarsmen—we watched the races that began with the *pupparini,* the sleek boats rowed by kids whose speed I admired.

"Come," Papa shouted. "Now to the judges' stand!"

I ran hard, keeping up only because of my longer legs, for he had stronger wind and stamina. Together we zigzagged our way through the crowd to the turning point at Santa Lucia Railway Station, the point they say the crowd can tell who will win—and this my father did, shouting to the oarsmen for he knew them all by name as they raised their oars in victory before the *macchina*, the floating stage moored in front of *Ca'Foscari* where they received their pennants.

So vivid is this memory, I am startled by the whining of the pups who noisily protest. "But, Mama, you promised!"

"Yes, I did, and I am sorry. But today I can't."

Wearily I climb down from the loft. "I'll take them."

"You can handle four pups?"

"Three," says Aldo from his corner where he lies facing the wall.

"Four," I say knowing that for the sake of my little brother, I must force myself from this depression. So, lifting him, I move toward the door with the others nipping at my legs.

Isabella nods toward the wicker basket by the door. "Take it."

"I won't need it," I reply with the pups shooting out into the street. Isabella raises her brow but does not look up as she grates the horseradish more forcefully, and I do indeed wonder what I have gotten myself into. With Aldo in my arms, I chase after the pups who are heading toward San Elena Gardens where the races have already begun. In a loose pack, we make our way through the back alleys and over the *rio terrà* to the place where from all directions the pedestrians are spilling like streams into a river.

Everywhere I turn my head is joy and celebration while in the cavern of my chest, my heart howls at the loss of my father. Also grieving, Aldo sighs, oblivious to his siblings who bark, begging from the locals and tourists who happily toss them all sorts of treats. And then from behind comes a stranger who claps me on the back and spins me around to clasp my paw between his thick, calloused hands. I wheel around to face an oddly familiar stranger with silver tufts spouting from a set of large ears.

"I knew your father from the time he was as young as those pups."

"I'm sorry, have we met?"

"Yes, Piccolo. On your return to Venice, don't you recall? I'm Gian Carlo."

"Ah, yes, my father's friend." We embrace and Aldo squirms, annoyed to be caught between us.

"Sometimes there are no words, Piccolo. But know I am close to your pain."

I bow my head. "Thank you for your condolences, Gian Carlo."

"Alfonso Fortunato will always be my friend, some things not even death can change."

"Yes," I agree though in my heart I am not convinced.

"Did you know your papa used to work for me? He wasn't much older than you when he came to me for a job. And he was the best assistant I ever had. And I am not saying that because he was your papa."

"I didn't know my father ever had a job."

"Well, you know artists, a very independent bunch, eh? But this was when he had first met his sweetheart over by the Rialto and he wanted to earn some money to make a little love nest for his new bride."

"I didn't know any of this."

"What do any of us know of our parents and their lives before we busted onto the scene."

"So, what did he do?"

"What else would we do—we cooked! He'd scratch at my door each morning before eight, and we'd walk together to the market. He had an amazing nose for the freshest fish, and the ripest vegetables rolled right into his paws. And being a sculptor, he had the most amazing knife skills." Gian Carlo pauses. "Hey, Piccolo, how about you?"

"What about me?"

"Want a job?"

I think about it. Afterall, Papa spent the last of our money on that case of Prosecco, and I absolutely do not want to become a burden on my mother who has enough to handle with her brood.

"Yes, I do need a job."

"Then meet me, Piccolo, tomorrow eight o'clock on the Rialto."

"Yes, Gian Carlo, I will."

I embrace the man who smells of cephalopods and old wool. Then in the doorway of a nearby building, a female of an older age waves to him, the lowness of the neckline of her lace dress revealing the fullness of her teats. Gian Carlo tosses back his head and tips his cap. "Well, help yourself so that God will help you," he says striding toward the woman who with one hand on her hip, smiles in a way that both chides and forgives. I observe the hug with which he enwraps the lady standing on tiptoes in her house slippers, then look around for the three pups who are nowhere in sight.

In an instant my reverie gives way to horror at having lost Isabella's babies. My eyes search the quay and scan the boats along its edge where spectators applaud the passing gondoliers.

"Aldo, your brothers. They're gone."

Still sleepy the pup yawns and squints. "Gone where?"

"Just gone."

I hurry through the crowd, my nostrils twitching in search of that distinct smell of puppy breath and pink bellies.

Aldo yaps sharply, but the sound of his voice is absorbed by the clapping and shouts of the crowd. I hold my brother aloft to be better heard until their overlapping yips and yaps arise from someplace close by, muffled by the snacks they are chewing.

"Brother, over there!"

I prick up my ears and detect that they are just a few steps away at the vaporetto station where service workers watch the race, and one woman shares her lunch with the hungry pups.

"More, signora, more!"

Though I scold the pups for running off, they ignore me while ravaging the meat off the carcass of a roasted chicken. Aldo and I exchange the glance that says barbarians as the woman holds out a lamb chop to me but feeling no appetite, I give it to Aldo who eats it in my arms as we walk along, seeking an open space where we can view my favorite race. It is the women's twin oared *Mascarte*, the same race of long ago when the courtesans of our city, those bold businesswomen, competed to win the admiration of all Venice. Today the women are rowing their sleek boats with much concentration as from the quay I enjoy the pure line of their torsos, like classical sculptures come to life in white t-shirts and pink sweatbands.

While their boats glide out of sight, I lead the pups along the route that my father and I used to take to reach the finish line to cheer for the winners who raise their oars in triumph. Along with the unruly pups, I tilt my muzzle skyward and howl with the crowd, forgetting for a moment who is not with me. But now that the pups are beginning to stumble with tiredness, I wish I had taken Isabella's advice and brought the basket. Nudging them along when they flop against a cistern or doorstep to rest, I slowly make my way toward Giuseppe's shed where Isabella waits nervously at the door.

"Finally, Piccolo! I was beside myself."

"Isabella, please, you had no need to worry. I am full grown."

"Yes, I have heard that often from you and your brother, but like him in many ways you are still a pup."

I mutter as I climb up to the loft. "Yes, a pup as long as I remain under this roof." Below in his corner Aldo sets the needle of the record player on an album with an American version of the *Three Penny Opera.* I paw the blanket and circle three times before I settle down into a sleep as deep and empty as a hole.

Each morning I rise early to make my way to the Ponte di Rialto, arriving at the market as the stevedores unload barges and vendors lay out the wide-eyed fish on trays of ice, the cephalopods and shellfish, the mollusks still sleek with the briny moisture of the lagoon. The merchants chat easily with me, exchanging bits of news on the Rialto while I await Gian Carlo's arrival to walk through the Pescaria discussing the day's menu.

As we make our selections, the vendors weigh our purchases that shimmer on the scales in the morning light. Moving through the stalls of the *Erberia*, I admire the brash fruits and vegetables that rival the walls of any museum for color and composition, but the market being more pleasurable because here I can bite into a sample of a stunningly fresh work of art.

With our cart full, we stop for an espresso and pastry, my

favorite being a warm *tortino di riso* filled with rice pudding and fresh from the oven. Our stomachs full and spirits lifted, we head back to our kitchen where each day the maestro teaches me new culinary techniques. Those foods that have bewitched me since childhood are no longer a mysterious act of nature, but the reward of a well-practiced craft. I learn to pound and blend the salt cod with olive oil and beat it with a wooden spoon into a frothy mousse—ah, the baccalà mantecato. I also learn to simmer and stir the risotto in the black ink of the squid to delectable perfection, and above all I master the art of making the polpette that had been my father's favorite. Told by many customers that mine are best in Venice, I at first attribute their remarks to the wine and warmth of Gian Carlo's comradery, but as I observe their eyes flutter when they take that first bite, I begin to take pride in the praise. In addition, I am assured by Gian Carlo, who has purchased one of their electronic devices that he checks throughout the day, that our polpette are receiving excellent reviews and many stars on Yelp and other sites on their internet.

At closing time Gian Carlo always fills a bag with crostini and many tasty bites for when I return to Giuseppe's shed where no matter how late, I am sure to be assaulted by the ravenous pups. With a laugh, I toss them the bag while I join Isabella at the table to watch Aldo perform the songs he has been practicing throughout the day—*Mack the Knife* having become his most recent favorite.

One night I notice that Aldo has taken my father's pork pie hat and claimed it as his own, so I ask Isabella for her sewing basket and from it I take her scissors, needle and a spool of thread. I clip the hat band and tailor it to fit his head. From that day forward, Isabella tells me that he will not leave the shed for the Piazza without it. And that throughout the day he wears it, tilting it left, right, forward and placing it jauntily on the back of his head as he sings a medley of songs from Papa's records to an admiring crowd. Being proud, she does not allow him to pass around the hat for donations—although she does admit seeing a surge in sales for her watercolors, enabling her to not only buy a heater for the shed, but to allow Giuseppe to semi-retire, switching from working full-time to three days a week.

If anyone had asked me in August how I would survive the loss of my father—I would have had no answer. But late summer has given way to autumn and soon after winter, with my routine of working six days out of seven sustaining me. Whether chopping, frying or serving, wiping down tables or taking cash, I never think beyond the moment—the pop of the cork, the clatter of dishes, the pleasant patter of voices, the clink of their raised glasses and the sound of the cash register drawer. By December I feel an urge to live again.

One afternoon while walking along the Riva degli Schiavoni, I look toward the lagoon where the cold air that has rolled down the snowy mountaintops on the mainland mingles with the salty water to create a mist that makes my Venice behind her veil even more elusive and beautiful.

At this time, Chiara comes to my mind, framed by the doorway of Anna's bedroom, her sad eyes peering out from a skull as well-carved as any ancient sculpture chiseled by the creator from stone. Cold air rushes into my lungs, bracing me with a hope that yes, all things are possible, and that one day I might lure her from her sorrow and together create a life that I can only vaguely imagine.

"Piccolo!"

I turn to see a jogger lumbering toward me, the mist rising from his open mouth with each icy exhalation and am surprised to see my large friend moving toward me. "Francesco!"

"Yeah, I know," he says between breaths, leaning forward with his gloved hands on his knees. "Me, running, not my thing. But I've got to drop a couple of pounds."

"Well, it is very pleasant to see you."

"You too. I was wondering when I'd bump into you again. What have you been up to?"

"Cooking, making cicchetti at a place over in Dorsoduro."

"Nice. Listen, I got to keep moving, but what are you doing Friday?"

"Friday?"

"Yeah, Christmas Eve. Come by my place."

I shake the woolen mitten that encases his hand as the other clasps my shoulder. "Yes, I would like that. I would like that very much."

"And bring Isabella and the pups."

"We'll see," I reply thinking to myself that I could use a few hours away from the shed without them. "And, oh, by the way," I say trying to sound nonchalant. "Have you heard from New York. You know, from Chiara, I mean, Anna."

"Yeah, they're doing great, found a place near Columbia, right next to the park. Anna sends her regards. So, yeah, see you Friday. Gotta keep moving." And breathing heavily, Francesco runs off at a speed that others walk.

I think of Chiara living in that faraway place—and like the rise and fall of the tide that erodes the bricks that shore up our city, the brief happiness I had felt at the thought of her now recedes with the truth that we might never meet again. And like the brickwork, I feel myself begin to crumble.

But this time I shake myself firmly from the tip of my nose to the tip of my tail and say to myself, "Get a grip on yourself, man, forget her. At least for now."

And so, I step into a crowded bàcaro where at the counter I first point to the crostini smeared with gorgonzola and anchovies, but it being a winter day, I also go for the veal *stracotto* on a crusty roll and order an ombra of red wine to wash it all down. Quickly I demolish the food and lap up the heavenly sauce from the stew with such force that the small plate falls to the floor and breaks in three pieces. Having already paid, I slip out through a side door into the alley, feeling a bit sheepish but revived and resolved to enjoy my day off.

With nowhere in particular to go, I stroll aimlessly, passing a shop window stacked with bolts of fabric and spindles of sequin where an old woman on her knees is decorating with fresh fir branches and strands of green ribbon. With her silver hair and gentle features, she looks like *la Befana*, the good witch who brings presents on the Epiphany. And with her lipstick seeping into the fine lines around her mouth, she smiles up at me as she plugs in a strand of tiny white lights that ignite in my mind a burst of images of holidays past.

Watching her set down the figurines of shepherds, sheep, one cow and an ass around the empty manger, I recall how we three would walk to the Church of San Felice on Christmas Eve.

There Papa would leave us at the stone steps and return after midnight Mass when together we would stroll home. After a few minutes in the kitchen, Mama would emerge carrying a plate with thick slices of *panettone*. And between bites of the sweet bread studded with bits of candied fruit, I would beg until she relented and gave me my gifts to unwrap. Being both Christmas and my birthday, there were always two—a new tool for making sculpture and a book to add to our Tintin collection that I would read several times before dawn.

I am drawn back to the present by the tapping on the glass. It is la Befana who wishes me *buon Natale* before unfolding herself from the narrow window and returning into her shop. Stepping into the vestibule, I open the door over which a brass bell rings. "And a good Christmas to you, la Befana." I smile at her and feel for the first time that my expression is not the superficial grin I so often give them, but it has a warmth that radiates from within.

Now I am resolved. With the money that I have saved from my job, I will go buy gifts for Isabella and her babies and find something special for my little brother. Hurrying back to the shed, I creak open the door and greet Isabella who raises a spoon to her muzzle. "Shush, they're sleeping."

Careful not to disturb our peace by waking the pups, I climb the steps and creep into the loft where, tucked under my folded blanket I keep the wallet that had once been fat with Mason's kitchen money, but now holds the cash I have earned in recent months from my job. But where will I find a suitable gift for Isabella? Kitchenware, a bottle of perfume, even a box of sweet torrone studded with almonds—all seem so inadequate for a female of such pedigree.

I am about to set off on my search when Mama motions for me to join her by the stove where she is frying a mix of scallops, squid and sardines. But when she leans toward me to kiss me goodbye, I steal a golden bite from the *frito misto*. Playfully, she takes her slotted spoon still hot from the oil and touches my paw—a quick burn that doesn't stop me from popping the pillowy scallop between my tongue and the roof of my mouth where I feel a second burn—the pleasure of the pain only intensified by the taste of the succulent flesh at the center of its crispy battered edge. Even more enjoyable is the expression on Mama's face, that look that says I am impossible but that she loves me without measure.

I nudge her affectionately with my snout before slipping back outside to hurry to the *Corte dei Miracoli.* Where better to look for Isabella's gift than at the open-air flea market where table after table is laden with random treasures? It was here she would take me once a year after Mass to shop for a present for her sister in Naples.

Although in childhood they had been separated after the sudden death of their father, the sisters remained close. And here Isabella would stroll through the courtyard, her creamy coat aglow in the soft light of a winter afternoon, chatting with merchants while she selected my aunt's gift.

As a pup I was bored by the shopping, but as an artist I now admire the visual opulence: crystal wine goblets rimmed in gold, a bundle of letters bound by a silk ribbon, a bowl of buttons, stacks of books bound in leather, many moldy from the moist air, and then on a mirrored tray I see a silver brush with a filigree edge—its bristles pale yellow with age. I lift it, then brush the fur along my leg and marvel at its softness.

"Bad dog," snarls the hag whose mouth is pinched and twisted. "Put that down."

My eyes narrow and I bare my teeth. "How much?"

"Oh, and you have money to pay?"

"How much," I say unfolding my wallet.

"For you," she pauses to eye my cash. "Twenty euros."

I peel off a bill from the stack and toss it on the table. "And for you? Ten is plenty."

"How dare you," she sneers as she sweeps the money into the pocket of her apron. By her side sits a tired old man on a folding chair who stares blankly at the air before him, probably numbed by decades of her complaints. Reaching into a shoebox beside him on the ground, he pulls out a plastic bag which he holds out to me.

"Let him carry it in his teeth." The hag snatches it from his hand and wags a crooked finger in my face. "Now you go."

"Take that dried up finger out of my face, or I will be carrying it off in my teeth."

"Hmph." The witch is silenced by the insult as the old man vaguely smiles.

Stopping before the church of *Santa Maria dei Miracoli,* I examine the hairbrush. Enjoying the feel of the cold silver against my paw and turning it slowly, I am admiring its workmanship when I notice the swirling initials engraved on its handle: I. F. It is now I know that just as I have been searching for the perfect gift for Isabella Fortunato, the silver brush has been waiting for me.

And then a thought sparks in my brain.

Just as Papa used to speak of the kinship of all species, perhaps on earth all things are similarly connected. That all creation is meant to be admired—even its raw materials, shaped into useful forms that in turn must be valued—not used and tossed off like a dirty napkin which itself having purpose should be honored. That indeed there is on earth a kinship of all things.

Then recalling Papa's religion, I utter a quick prayer skyward. "Grazie."

"You're' welcome," replies a middle-aged woman who is swollen with must be a litter of at least three pups in her belly. She sits and strings colorful beads with a long needle along a nylon thread. "And perhaps there is some pretty trinket here that will make your sweetheart say thank you, eh?" She grins with a mouth that flaunts more empty spaces than teeth.

I dip my paw into one of the many clear bowls filled with cool glass beads "I wish." If I had not already bought the brush, I might have selected one of the gleaming necklaces or sets of dangling earrings that hang from a rack. But I do consider purchasing a long-stemmed rose, each petal sewn from a hundred tiny globes.

"How much?"

"Two for one, three for five."

"I'll take one."

"Ah, your sweetie will be touched by your taste, if not by your generosity," says the woman as I pay her two euros.

Ignoring her sarcasm, I tell her I am looking for another gift. "For my, uh, nephews." I am hesitant to call them brothers but being their Zio Piccolo, nephews feels appropriate.

"Boys. You've got to keep them busy, tire them out." She puts aside her beadwork and with some effort to lift her considerable girth, she reaches behind the table for a green and white box which she hands to me. I feel the roundness of the ball that protrudes from the packaging.

"A football, perfect. How much?"

"I got it for five, I'll give it to you for six."

"Six? That is too cheap. I'll give you seven."

"You are a strange dog," she says reaching out for the money with one hand and bracing her back with the other. "But I never argue over money. God bless you, mister."

"And you too, mother."

"And here, I'll toss this in." She hands me a drawstring

laundry bag in which I place my purchases. Tossing it over my back, I continue in search of one more perfect gift for Aldo until beneath the only tree in the square, I am distracted by a rack of vintage men's clothing. Pushing aside each hanger along a steel bar, I admire the fabric and style of each garment, particularly intrigued by the interlocking black and white pattern of one vest.

From between two pairs of trousers a big-nosed head emerges. "Nice houndstooth."

"Thank you, I do on occasion brush and floss."

"No, not your teeth, the fabric. The pattern, it's call houndstooth."

"Ah, I see."

"Try it on."

"Me?"

"Yeah, sure, why not? You're a dashing dog."

When he steps from behind the rack, he takes the vest from the hanger and holds it open, but I step aside.

"Go ahead, try it on."

The cool silk lining slides over my back, and when the merchant points toward a full-length mirror, I step before the antique frame and admire the look of the vest on my body.

"Suits you, pup," he says in a voice so familiar and friendly that I take no offense to his use of the word.

"How much?"

"Fifteen."

"Twelve," I shoot back as I used to hear my mother haggle in this way.

"Thirteen fifty."

"Sounds fair."

I pay the vendor and walk away, proud to have bought my first article of clothing. For a working dog, few pleasures rival buying the goods you desire with the cash you have earned. I know that the wealthy need only awake each morning to find their money morphed into greater and greater masses—but I wonder if they can feel the same satisfaction. And how valuable can those gifts be when paid for by profits on investments earned by others? For me, I want the gift I give to bear the imprint of my sweat. And on that day in the flea market, I feel that pride fully, wearing my houndstooth vest and carrying in my bag the soft-bristled brush for my mother, the beaded rose and the football for her pups.

Still searching for a gift for Aldo, I come to a table lined with milk crates of records and CDs when from a battered pair of speakers emerges a voice as honest as a friend and as lovely as the flakes of snow that have begun to fall. The song is *Bianca Natale*, and it is sung by Andrea Bocelli, the boy from Tuscany who grew up to become the man of the world. As I stand flipping through the records, I come across some Blue Note albums that Aldo has already inherited from my father's collection. Then I feel the thrill of the hunt when I come across a record with a faded cover. It is a 1930s recording of songs by Cole Porter, the American composer who Papa told me once lived in Ca'Rezzonico, the palazzo on the Grand Canal where he hired a hundred servants and a troupe of tightrope walkers to entertain his guests. I take the vinyl from the paper sleeve and examine it for scratches and am pleased to find very few.

A guy in a sweat suit glances up as he counts the cash in a cigar box. "I see you appreciate the oldies." The merchant points his scruffy chin toward a crate of VHS boxes at the far end of the table. "How about some vintage films?" I turn my attention to the box in which are stacked many of the same movies I used to watch with Papa that were later destroyed by flooding in our ground floor room.

For Aldo I select the best—*E.T.*, *Rocky 1* and *3*, two Chaplin films and Vittorio De Sica's *Bicycle Thief*. After bargaining with the vendor, I pack all the gifts into my sack and indeed feel like the white-bearded *Babbo Natale* as I head home from the market. Fortunately, Mama is out with the pups when I arrive back at the shed, and so I zip open my duffel bag and stow away the gifts.

That week passes quickly as Christmas approaches, and as is my routine, each morning I meet Gian Carlo on the Rialto, returning to his place to work throughout the day, taking only one break each afternoon when I tuck my apron under the counter and hurry out of the shop.

Running across the Ponte dell'Accademia toward San Marco, I always arrive at three o'clock to pull the cart with Mama's pictures and the bickering pups back home for the pain in her injured leg has worsened in the damp winter air.

On this day heading back to Dorsoduro, I make a second stop to check on Iona who stands where the crane of the UPS barge had placed her on the quay—not far from the two giant columns on top of which are Saint Theodore and the lion of San Marco. Like most Venetians I do not walk between them. In my case, I am not superstitious, but out of respect for the prisoners who in the 18th century were hung at this site. But on this late afternoon it is as if I feel the heaviness of their souls suspended somewhere between Venice and the hereafter—whatever that might be. And though my father raised me to be a rational creature, I find myself staring at the grey whorls of mist that roll over the Pizzetta, perplexed by their source and the dark thoughts they bring to my mind.

Standing beside Iona, I crane my neck to better see the saint who stands holding his shield and spear above a slain crocodile—that reptile that my father taught me was a symbol of despair. Then turning my attention to the top of the other column where a seagull perches atop the winged lion, I recall his words. "The lion, Piccolo, is courage. And if in your mind, you find yourself standing between the two, choose courage over despair, and you will always triumph."

But Iona being carved of wood has no such principle to sustain her, and the moist air having seeped into her cracks, her wood is on the verge of splitting. I worry how to save this work of art as I have neither a studio nor a way to convey her to a dry space to make the necessary repairs. And so, each day the tracks of termites and other boring insects lengthen, and Iona inches her way closer to becoming mulch.

I am about to head back to the bàcaro when intuition tells me to stop. I then hear the motor of a boat and turn to see the green barge approaching. It stops beside the place on the quay where Iona stands, extending its crane to hover above her as a city worker leaps from the deck to secure crisscrossing straps about her form. For a moment, I stand paralyzed, then run to the edge of the canal and bark as Iona rises like a ponderous and silent angel.

"Wait," I call to the pilot of the barge. "You are mistaken. Iona, she is mine."

"You got a permit?"

"I don't understand."

"What's not to understand? This is a public space. You need a permit for a statue."

"Oh, but Iona, she is so much more than a statue. She is my last link."

"Listen, my friend, I'm just doing a job here." The worker unstraps Iona and returns to the controls to drive the barge out to sea.

Where is he taking her? To dump her on a landfill with junked cars, computer parts and copious piles of plastic where seagulls squawk fighting over a shred of food in that heap of trash. Or will he simply push her overboard into the lagoon? I much prefer the second scenario as she will fall once and deeply to be preserved in the salty water, but on land the process of disintegration will take decades, maybe a hundred years. Time. It had taken months for my spark for life to be rekindled, which in a few minutes has been doused with the cold reality that a dog without a permit—nor money for a bribe—can even attempt to rescue an irreproducible work of art.

As I walk, the lights in the square, the singing of the carolers have no effect on me. In a daze I return to the shed and push open the door. And although the air is fragrant with the broth of carrots, herbs and onions, not even the aroma of the Christmas rooster simmering on the range, can uplift my sunken spirit.

Then I see the pups bouncing the football while Aldo sits with his nose almost touching the screen watching Charlie Chaplin's little tramp. With a quick and guilty glance, Isabella looks at me and hides something behind her back.

"My gifts. Why are my gifts out?"

"Oh, Piccolo. I was preparing the *brodo di caponne,* and when I turned around the boys were already rummaging through your sack."

"And what of you? You don't have any self-control either?"

"Piccolo, that is so unfair," she says, placing the silver hairbrush on the table.

As Isabella reaches for the wooden pin and rolls out the dough on the floured table, I feel ashamed. "I'm sorry, Isabella. It's just that nothing goes the way I plan."

"Be careful what you affirm, son. If you tell the universe nothing, it will give you nothing. But if you rejoice, the universe gives you joy."

"Rejoice? Rejoice in what?"

"In whatever you will achieve through your own goodwill and stubborn effort," she says taking a small cup and pressing it down on the dough.

"What, working in a kitchen? Coming back to a shed I share with four pups as if I am too still a child?"

"Look inside, son, and see your true self and your true desire—tell me, what is in your heart?"

And before I can stop myself from uttering her name it springs from my lips. "Chiara."

"Then pursue Chiara wherever life takes you."

Stunned by the challenge of her words, I have no response. I stand and watch her cut out the round shapes from the thin dough for the *cappelletti,* the stuffed pasta she will serve tomorrow after Mass for lunch along with the *ossocollo*—the rustic sausage that she has set on a high shelf far from the reach of the pups that even in these hard times she will serve on her simple table as will the wealthiest Venetians. "For in life you must find your own way."

"I don't even know where to look."

"I know you can't live here with us forever. You must have your own friends, your own life and a future. Italy's hand is tight-fisted and offers nothing to her children. Anna explained it to me. Maybe it will be in pursuing Chiara that you will find your path."

"I will try."

"Don't try, son. Do." Isabella shakes the rolling pin at me. "You know, I met Francesco in the marketplace today, and he invited us to his party."

I say nothing as I have no intention of going to the gathering with all of them.

"I told him that we couldn't make it, but that you would be there. Afterall, you are looking very sharp in your new vest."

I smile self-consciously, watching her dip her spoon into the mix of parmesan, ground sausage, and nutmeg. With delicacy she fills, then pinches and seals the edge of the dough.

"Please, Mama," I beg with my tail wagging wildly.

"Piccolo, no meat tonight. These are for tomorrow."

"Please, Mama. Just one."

"Okay, hush, just don't tell the others." She slips a half dozen dumplings into the simmering broth of the capon. I stand there, mesmerized by their movement in the boiling water, waiting for the plump little darlings to rise to the surface.

Finally, she dips her ladle into the pot, splashing the steaming *brodo di cappelletti* into my bowl. First, I slurp, then bite down on the hot morsel that explodes with its flavor, searing my mouth—no, not its flavor, but the flavor of all the cappelletti I have eaten over the course of all the Christmases since my creation. I feel the stress of my self-doubt melt away and in its place I feel the joy of basic living. "*Santo Natale*, son, and may your blessings be many, and your troubles be few."

While Isabella begins singing that Christmas song so reminiscent of my childhood, my little brother joins in just as I did as a pup. I sneeze with great emotion, launching a little dumpling across the room which lands in Aldo's open mouth. His jaws snap down on the unexpected snack, and for the first in many years, I hear Isabella laugh.

"Now go, Piccolo. And enjoy Francesco's party."

"I'm ready," says Aldo who with his pork pie tilted jauntily on his head, grabs Mama's cane from the corner, then waddles toward the door, mimicking the pigeon-toed walk of Charlie Chaplin's little tramp whose movies Aldo has been watching on the VCR all day.

"No, not tonight. Piccolo needs some time on his own."

Aldo's eyes widen, his brow furrows and he begins to whimper.

"Okay, okay, you can come. But let's get out of here before the others notice."

Isabella wraps a handknitted scarf around Aldo's neck, then closes and bolts the door behind us. The air is crisp, and many store windows are framed with fir branches and the passageways are lit with strands of bulbs. But even brighter are the smells on that night of all nights in Cannaregio—where from the open windows of my neighbors' kitchens we are greeted by the aroma of every creature procreated in our lagoon—grilled, fried, roasted and boiled in honor of *la Vigilia.*

"Ah, Christmas eve, Aldo, is the finest night of the year."

"Why, big brother?"

"Because on this night hope is pure and innocence possible, and that Aldo is the great gift of this holiday."

"And the *pandoro*."

"Ah, yes, the Christmas cake."

We trot along the Strada Nova, but then taking a shortcut through a narrow alley, we emerge into an unfamiliar courtyard, and then an unfamiliar street. And I am lost in my own city.

"Brother, are we almost there?"

"In Venice we are always almost there, but the question is which way?"

Aldo points toward a silvery mist. "Ask her."

"Who? I see no one."

"There, the white dog."

"What white dog?"

"The one that just ran down that alley."

Having no better plan, I go in the direction that Aldo says the white dog has gone. As we emerge from an alleyway, Aldo points again. "There she is, crossing that bridge."

I feel foolish taking directions from a pup, yet something urges me to follow the dog I cannot see down streets I do not know. After a few minutes moving in blind faith, I sense familiarity.

"Ah, the Fondamente Nove."

"I knew she would lead us in the right direction."

"Who?"

"Her."

Aldo points again, this time toward a churning patch of silver mist that is crossing the lagoon toward San Michele, the island that Papa and I could see from Anna's balcony, the island that has been a cemetery for over two hundred years. Feeling a sudden icy chill, I enter the hallway with Aldo in my arms and climb the stairs, glad to hear the sounds of the living coming from Francesco's place.

We rise to the landing where Aldo leaps from my arms. Standing in the doorway, he tilts his hat and adjusts his scarf, observing the living room where Francesco's guests eat, drink and chat in many languages. But all sounds cease when Aldo enters. All eyes follow the chubby pup who waddles in, twirling his cane, stopping to raise his hat and wink at a long-haired female who wears a silky blue dress. A strand of sea pearls that rest on the swells of her breasts rise and fall with her laughter. She winks back and tosses him a sugary *zeppola* that he catches between his teeth causing an uproar in the room—which only grows louder with delight when Aldo hops onto the low table and breaks into the song that he has been practicing in the shed for weeks—*Mack the Knife.*

Francesco comes from the kitchen to give me a hug and kiss my cheek. "Oh, Piccolo, I am so glad you made it."

"Yes, thank you, my good friend. I am happy to be here."

"Come. Keep me company in the kitchen while I make the *anguilla*. Nice vest."

"Ah, the eels!"

"Wouldn't be Vigilia without them."

I follow him into the narrow kitchen and sit up on a high stool at the counter that faces the living room where Aldo flirts with the guests between songs—a repertoire of American classics he has learned from the vinyl albums from Alfonso's collection.

Francesco hands me a tall glass with a slice of blood orange twisted over its rim. When I hesitate to drink, he pours its contents into a bowl that he sets down on the counter. Sitting on the stool, I lean over to lap it up, my nose twitching at the bitterness of the herbs combatting the sweetness of the juice.

"Campari, to whet your appetite for the meal. But tell my, my friend, what's with the bowl? Everything else you do like a man, why lap up your drink like a dog?"

"Exactly that, Francesco, to remember. Because to forget would be to dishonor those who came before."

"Then let us drink to your ancestors," he says raising his glass.

"And to the kinship of all species," I add remembering my father's toast. Then to my surprise, all the guests raise their glasses and echo my words. "To the kinship of all species!" We drink deeply and when we set down our glasses, Aldo leads the crowd in the singing of *Bianca Natale* while Francesco returns to preside like Neptune with his full beard and shirt open to the waist over his creatures of the lagoon.

He opens the oven door to spill some wine over the eels, letting them roast for a few more minutes while at the sink he rinses the sea bass under running water before returning to the counter where he sets down bay leaf, sage and clove.

"Do you mind stuffing the *branzino?"*

"My pleasure." I move to the sink to wash up before preparing the fish.

Francesco then takes the eels out of the oven and piles them on a platter of grilled polenta that he adorns with wedges of lemon. Ah, the *risotto de peverasse*, studded with succulent clams. Even now my mouth waters at the memory of his simple, but exquisitely prepared meal. As each guest from the lagoon is cooked to perfection, I place the white platters on the long table that has been set up in the living room—exerting restraint to deliver each dish without slipping behind the door to ravish it alone.

With the arrival of the food, the noisy crowd grows silent—with only the sounds of oh and ah punctuating their chewing, looking up from their plates only to dip into the side dishes of vegetables and various dressings or to reach for a chilled bottle of Soave or Verdicchio to tilt over one another's glasses.

Francesco and I continue to cook and serve until finally we step up to the table where he fills my plate with a sample of each dish.

What happiness I feel that night, a happiness enhanced by the presence of these fine-looking strangers and watching them enjoy the food that I have served them. After they have returned to the table several times before falling back in surrender on the sofa, chairs and pillows strewn about the floor, I fill my plate again and slip into the bathroom where I close the door and eat with abandonment. Afterward I have to lay down on the cool tiles to digest—until someone knocks and in an urgent voice asks to use the room.

I return to the living room where the table has been cleared and the *dolci di Natale* are being brought from the kitchen by the girl in the blue dress. Beside the trays of pastries and cakes, Francesco sets down three bottles of a yellowy-green liquid that I stare at with curiosity.

"That's the limoncello, I bottled it myself." Francesco pulls out the cork with his flat teeth and pours a drink into my bowl. Although I know I should probably drink no more as I will have to carry Aldo home, I cannot resist the zesty smell of lemon nor the light sweetness that goes so well with the *cantuccini*, the twice-baked biscotti and the small cup of tortoni topped with a cherry that Aldo's new friend has placed on my plate.

Although I am aware that in the presence of so many lovely ladies, my stomach is bulging from beneath my vest, I cannot resist a spoonful of ice cream laced with almond. Finally sated, I climb on the couch no longer tempted by the vast array of sweets, not even the *tronchetto di Natale*, the swirling yellow cake that folds over the mocha cream, collapsing under a dark layer of thick chocolate.

"What's that?" Aldo asks.

"That's the Yule log," says the girl in blue as she cuts a fat slab for the puppy who watches its approach transfixed.

Approaching with a spoon, I warn her. "Though tempting, our species can't consume chocolate."

Francesco laughs, "Ah but, Piccolo, you have adapted so well to the wine!"

"After all, my friend, I may be a greyhound, but I am still Italian!"

Aldo sighs as I scoop off the ganache, but when the girl sets the plate before him, he pushes his muzzle into the soft mound of sweetness and does not lift his head until it is devoured. Then finally from the exhaustion of all the eating and singing, my little brother falls asleep with his head resting on her wide and comfortable thigh as she strokes him under the chin.

As some guests leave and others fall asleep, Francesco nods toward the kitchen and whispers, "I have saved something for us."

From a high shelf in his cabinet, he takes down a narrow crate and slides open the top to reveal a bottle packed in curling slivers of thin wood. "McCallan." Francesco raises one eyebrow in what I think might be both admiration and invitation, but I am not sure. "Single malt scotch whiskey."

I recall with mild nausea that night on the ship when Guy Gizárd introduced me to his friend Jack Daniels.

"Ah, Francesco, I have drunk so much already."

"But Piccolo, I have saved the best for last for us. This whisky has been aging for twelve years waiting for you to take a taste."

How can I reject such hospitality? And so, I join him at the counter. "Twelve years ago my grandfather was working in the boatyard of the Tramontin family, and my father would have been a pup, playing among the wood chips."

"History in a bottle," says Francesco, pouring us both a drink.

Leaning over my bowl, I discern the various components of its complex aroma. "Interesting. I smell the oak from the barrel and the fruitiness of perhaps plums, but something else?"

"Nutmeg."

"No, more like a layer of fragrant moss and moist clover that must be plentiful in the land it was distilled."

"What a nose you have, Piccolo, may it always keep you out of trouble and lead you ever closer to your happiness."

"And to you my good friend." I take a sip of the whisky that warms me. "May this new year lead you to your own success."

"My success," he says, but with a look I have trouble reading—something between chagrin and anger. Instinctively I pull back.

"Success in Italy? Not possible. With unemployment at thirty percent and rising? Where my degree can barely earn me a thousand a month. And with the way things are going, ten years from now, a thousand a month won't be a nightmare, it will be the dream."

Even in my inebriated state, I understand his frustration as I too was exploited in that Brooklyn studio. But I also understand the love and loyalty owed to our city.

"But Venice, Francesco, to her we must be faithful."

"Venice? Venice is a tramp."

Like a coil has sprung inside me, I leap with full force on his chest, pushing him to the ground where he looks at me with rage and confusion.

"You serious? You want to fight me?" He rises to his feet and towers above me like the Colossus.

Coming to my senses, I lick his clenched fist. "Francesco, forgive me. I am sorry. But the insult, the insult to our mother."

"Venice, Piccolo? Is she ours? With what, like sixty thousand of us left and more moving to the mainland every day? And what the tourists, like twenty million every year? Who does she exist for—us or them?"

"Venice exists for herself."

"Nice thought, Piccolo, but Venice is an amusement park. Cruise ships, four and five a day, spitting out tens of thousands of them with their selfie sticks and wheelie suitcases. They buy a mask and tell the world they know Venice. It's insane."

"But, ah, my friend, I have met many in the Piazza who are of a more respectful nature. They are not all curs."

"Perhaps, but just once I would like to walk around my own city without tripping over their pull along luggage or being blocked by a bunch of tourists clogging up a bridge or gawking at menus."

I sigh and look away sorry that I have lashed out at my friend, and also that what Francesco says is true. Sensing my sadness, he rubs my neck.

"But, Francesco, Venice was much revered by the masters. By Bellini, Tintoretto, Monteverdi, Vivaldi and countless others."

"And in their day, all were paid for their time and talents. Believe me, today? Would they even be able to pay the rent on their studios—would they even have the time to develop their talent, or would they be hawking souvenirs? Like me, they'd be gearing up to go."

"You, Francesco? You are leaving Italy?" I feel a tightness in my chest, the pain of losing Francesco, so soon after having lost my father is too much.

"Next week, right after New Year. I have a flight booked for Anchorage." He pours himself another whisky.

"And where is this Anchorage?"

"Alaska."

"Ah, the frigid regions described by my favorite author Jack London."

"Yes, mine too. Ever since I was a kid."

"There was a man who understood the heart of the dog."

"And the heart of the worker, but today you and I Piccolo are one in the same."

"Always we have survived side by side, even in the caves."

"And the caves are where we are headed again. But until we get there, I'll try my luck in Alaska."

"But why so far, Francesco?" I ask sad to lose my friend to that cold and distant place.

"A friend of mine from Palermo lives there, and he has a couple of fishing boats. He'll pay me good money and then in a few months, maybe a year, I'll move to New York and try to get an internship with an architectural firm."

"To be an intern? I am sorry, Francesco, but you must aim higher than that. You must be paid for your time, your talent, your education, your charisma!"

"Well, we'll see, my friend. But in the meantime, I will cast my nets in the sea and be rewarded with fish and a paycheck. And what of you, Piccolo, what is your plan?"

"For now, I will work with Gian Carlo."

"And what does he pay you for your time, your talent and your charisma?"

"He pays me what he can."

"And let me ask you this. Is it enough to move out of your mother's house?"

I lower my heard, too ashamed to answer.

"Then come with me, Piccolo. Come with me to Alaska, a dog of your caliber and with your skills in the kitchen, you will be welcome anywhere!"

"Honestly, with my thin coat we greyhounds are not well suited to the northern latitudes. But I have thought of travel."

"To where?"

"To the place Anna called Columbia, to be by the side…"

"Of Chiara."

"Yes, of Chiara."

"Then go to her. They have plenty of restaurants in New York, you can work there off the books and make good money with enough to send some home to your family."

I take another sip of the McCallan that warms my body along with the thought of Chiara. "Thank you, Francesco. But how could I know that she will even see me. And why go back to that pitiless city without that assurance?"

"Text her."

"What?"

"Well, text Anna. Let her know you're thinking about coming out there and see what she says."

"And what is this texting?"

"Oh, Piccolo, we have to get you a cell phone. It's a way of communicating in writing, especially if you don't want to talk directly to the person. This way if she says, yeah, they want to see you, great. And if it's no, well, nothing lost."

"Would you… text… for me?

"Sure, no problem." Francesco reaches for his electronic device on the counter and taps out the message.

"So, in how many days can we expect a reply?"

There is a buzz.

"That's probably her now."

I am astounded.

Francesco reads from the screen. "Merry Christmas to you and Piccolo. And yes, we'd love to see him." He holds out the phone for me to view a flat yellow face surrounded by hearts. "That's an emoji."

I am unimpressed by the moronic face, but deeply moved by the message. "They would love to see me?" I stutter less from the amount of alcohol I have consumed than from this instantaneous and favorable response.

"But how will I get there? And with what? The hundred or so I have saved?"

"Let me check something. I have a layover in New York." Francesco resumes tapping on his device.

"A lay… over?" The phrase brings to mind the imbecilic tricks that dogs are expected to perform like rolling over or playing dead—something I will do for no man, under no circumstance.

"A stop over, you know, the wait while the plane refuels, and the pilot gets a little blitzed." I tilt my head a little confused. "Says here for a fee, you can travel with me as a pet."

"Francesco, how can you even suggest such a thing?"

"I'm not asking you to be my pet. I'm just saying that it would be a cheap way for you to travel."

"I will consider your offer, Francesco, but if you will excuse me, I have to pee."

"You know where the bathroom is." He takes his empty glass and the bottle of whisky into the living room where several of his guests are sprawled out on the futon and the floor.

"Actually, I think I'll just go outside."

"Sure, I get it." Francesco sets down the glass and bottle and resting his head beside Aldo's on the blue folds of his new friend's lap, he too falls immediately to sleep. Careful not to wake them, I shut the door behind me and descend the stairs into the street.

The night is cold, but my mind is on fire with the possibility of traveling to New York in search of this place called Columbia to see again Chiara, to determine if in fact that powerful connection between us is real or imagined. As I lift my leg against the corner of the building, something white and fleeting catches my eye.

I bark in an ancient tongue from deep within that orders—stop and identify yourself.

And the hazy figure barks back—make me.

Clearly this is a challenge. And taking off my vest I accept—I'll race you.

And without a muscle's hesitation, we are off and running down the Fondamente Nove.

Though the white dog has an ample lead, I have the will of the contender—and with long strides we are soon neck and neck along the promenade when suddenly my opponent makes a sharp and unexpected turn down the Riva del Carbon, heading west.

My ears pressed back in the wind created by my speed, I feel fully alert and alive—with the muscles of my haunches powering each stride as one by one each paw hits the ground and lifts—front left, front right, back right, back left. And then catapulting forward, briefly airborne, I am certain in that moment that to be a greyhound is the greatest gift of all.

Clouds scuttle across the night sky as we approach the Ponte dell'Accademia where a group of revelers stop wide-eyed at our approach, falling back onto the wooden rails of the bridge, fumbling for their devices which they have no time to click for we have already hurtled past them.

Now the white dog has regained the advantage, setting the course of this race which intuition warns me might be leading me to danger. But I cannot dishonor the challenge of a race. And because this other dog is in the lead, I only gain in determination to see it through to the finish line—whether on earth or in the hereafter, we will cross it.

We approach another foot bridge, and I see our destination is Ca'Rezzonico. Energized by a preternatural burst of speed, I catch up to the white dog, and we finish this race with no winner. Gulping air and slightly dizzy from exertion, I face the dog who being of another realm has no need to pant.

Patiently this greyhound waits for me to catch my breath,

giving us both a moment to appraise one another—so similar in build and facial features that we might have been painted by the same brush. And I am struck by the familiarity of her gaze that reveals the same intelligence and humor that I recall from the portrait of my ancestor on my mother's side. Is this then her spirit, returned from the grave to challenge and to drive me to this place? But why?

When she turns and gives me a nod, I sense that I must follow. And although I'd like to linger on the first floor to study the paintings, sculptures and frescoed ceilings, she leads me without looking back to the grand staircase where for a moment I sit, hesitant to climb.

"Come." A voice commands from above.

On the landing of the second floor appears the faint figure of a man who like the dog gives off no smell. He wears a shimmering turban and motions for me to ascend the stairs. "Don't be afraid. Afterall, you have family here."

He smiles as he places his hand on the head of the greyhound who sits by his side and like him glows with a light from within.

Like lanterns they are leading me through the darkness when suddenly I catch sight of danger—a bird of prey—hawk or falcon I cannot tell, but at this moment it does not matter because clearly I can see its hooked talons aimed at my hide. My muscles tense. I bark to warn the homicidal bird that I will be no easy prey. I will fight.

The porous figure laughs aloud, and I am angered at the disrespect. "Look again. For what you fear is more pigment than predator."

And as I draw nearer to it, I see that the enemy I have so loudly challenged is a painted bird. Embarrassed I mumble something about the lack of light before following my hosts into the adjoining room.

When my eyes grow accustomed to the dark, I recognize this place that I visited often as a pup with Isabella. I can now make out the images of these frescoes—the *pulcinella*, those clowns of Venice as they tumble and carouse for the raucous crowd. I turn to see one fondle a woman's breast while another scratches his own behind.

"What do you think, my friend? Do you like these paintings?"

"Like? To like something is no more than a wag of the tail, an imbecile can like. But these paintings deserve much higher consideration. Perhaps if we have time, I can study them and find the words to describe their humor, their pathos, the artist's courage to put on canvas the foolishness and vulgarity of the species."

"This is an artist of much discernment," the phantom man says to the phantom dog who dips her head in agreement.

"I believed I was an artist until my father died. But now I am only the shell of who I had hoped to be."

"My father was an artist too, the greatest in his day. And when he died, for a time I felt the same as you. What was the point? I had been painting by his side since I was a boy—creating masterpieces for the kings of England and France, the Czarina of Russia. We painted in the courts of the Prince of Wurzburg Germany and the King of Spain. And then? He died. Suddenly. Gone."

We both sigh with the shared memory of our loss. "So, what did you do?"

"I returned to Venice, my place of peace and busied myself with the affairs of my villa on the mainland." Now the artist looks deeply into my eyes as if we are ancient friends. "And then one day I remembered who I am. And I prepared and painted the walls of our country house. And just as time was now my own, I could paint in my own way. Take this one."

He motions overhead to a lofty space that opens into the sky where a bunch of clowns swing from ropes.

"To my father's patrons, this one would have been a sacrilege. To put clowns in the heavens instead of them and their gods? But painting in my own home, for my own pleasure, I no longer had to

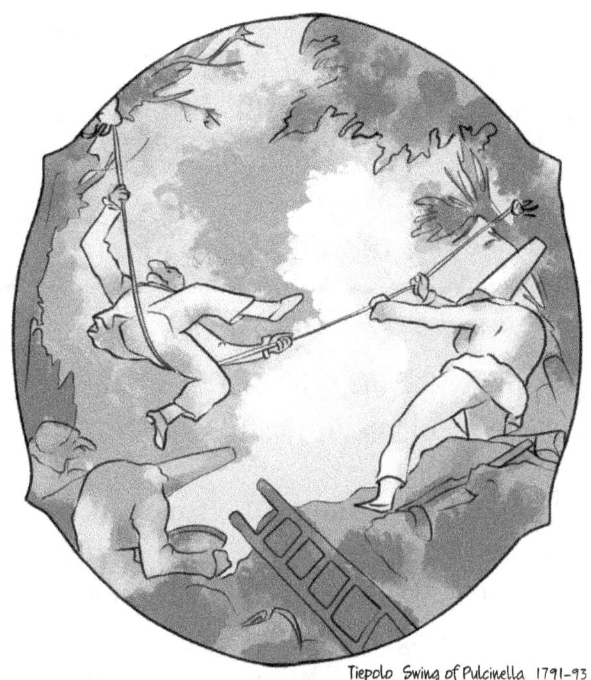

Tiepolo Swing of Pulcinella 1791–93

to care. At Zianigo I was free to paint as I chose—to see the universe with my own eyes to depict it in my own way—without myths and grandeur, from my own point of view. You see, Piccolo, I too lost my father, but to become truly an artist, I had to become my true self."

I am taken aback that the artist knows my name, but deeply moved by his message, I follow as he leads me to another canvas.

"And in this painting, you can see the world as I saw it. With this crowd crushed all together, all ages, all classes, gawking at the amusement of the Carnival that was called *il Mondo Nuovo*."

"And what was this new world?"

"Nothing but a box of illusion. Come closer. You see the one standing on the stool? Do you hear him calling out to all Venice?"

And pricking up my ears I can hear a distant voice arise from the canvas—Come one, come all, and see the New World!

"And they would come, as they always do to line up like fools,

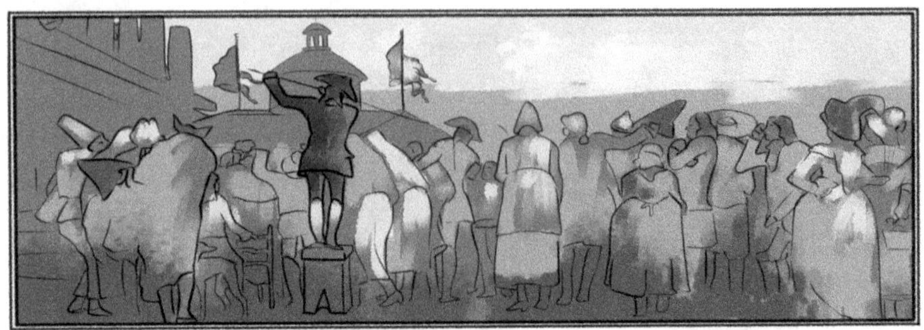

Tiepolo Mondo Novo 1791

pay their money and waste their time on an illusion. All are taken in by *il Mondo Nuovo*. All but the dog in the foreground who looks away."

I move closer to the painting to study the image of the greyhound, and by its intelligent expression, I see that my ancestor was its model. And as if she can read my thoughts, Tiepolo's greyhound gives me a single wag. I smile back, and when I think of the throngs of tourists in San Marco hypnotized by the devices of today, I realize how like her, I am not so easily taken in.

"But why do you paint them all from the rear?"

"I paint them from the back where there is no distinction between asses."

I laugh along with the painter, then read the bronze tag beside it to confirm what I have already surmised. That this indeed is the long dead son Giovanni Domenico Tiepolo, of the long dead dad, Giovanni Battista Tiepolo. And that my ancestor has drawn me to him to learn these lessons.

"Every loss creates a windy space to be filled. And whether gods or clowns run this show on earth, we must find dignity and meaning in what me make to ennoble our short lives."

Then as the sun inches over the Canal, a thin light enters the room and their figures fade, becoming as sheer as the curtains that hang over the long windows.

"Go, Piccolo, and be both the greyhound and the artist that you were born to be."

I touch my heart to check that it is still beating and relieved that I indeed still have a pulse, I watch in amazement as side-by-side Gian Domenico and his beloved greyhound, step out through the glass doors to merge with the mist over the Canalasso.

Both elated and fearing for my sanity, I am still lucid enough to know that I don't want to be found wandering around Ca'Rezzonico when the staff arrive. So, I hurry through the galleries and back down the stairs to the ground floor.

But as I pass through the portego, I must stop to pay homage to the workmanship of the 19th century gondola on display—the hand-carved *farcola* that steadies the oar; the metal work of the *ferro* at its prow—with its six gleaming bars a tribute to each of the *sestiere* of our city: San Marco, San Pollo, Santa Croce, Castello, Dorsoduro, and the district I will always call home Cannaregio.

Leaving Ca'Rezzonico, I feel the coolness of the marble tiles of the courtyard beneath my paws. And stepping outside into the early morning light, I admire my city—a tranquil beauty rudely awakened by some moron on the Ponte dell'Accademia flying a drone over the Grand Canal.

Trotting back to Francesco's place, I take the same route that I had raced the spirit of my ancestor through the night, but I am not the same. I know now who I am, and wherever life will lead me, I feel certain that as a greyhound and an artist, I will find my own way.

CODA

When I enter Francesco's building, the stairwell echoes with the voice of Aldo singing *From Rags to Riches,* crooning with all the frank passion of the great American singer Tony Bennet. But not until I enter the living room and see the delight with which the girl in the blue dress applauds my little brother, do I sense trouble.

"Come on, Aldo. Time to head home."

"I'm not going home."

"Excuse me?"

He shakes his head and replies with a yap.

"I don't understand."

"Dora has invited me to move in with her."

From the kitchen counter where she makes coffee, Dora waves. She speaks but I cannot make out her words over the rumble of the espresso maker as she heats the milk.

"Move in, Aldo? As in be her pet?"

"At least she will treat me with respect. Unlike my siblings who have belittled me since birth."

"And what will I tell Isabella?"

"Tell her we'll be by to pick up my movies."

I am overwhelmed that one so young can be so unfeeling but must respect my younger brother's decision—no matter how disastrous I think the consequences might be. Afterall, hadn't I done the same as a young dog myself?

Left with the task to break the news to Isabella, I return to Giuseppe's shed where she loudly and angrily blames me. But I understand. She is a mother, and as a mother she is under the mistaken belief that because she has fed her pups with her own milk, she must protect them beyond their weaning—a power that no male or female has to deflect their offspring from their own path.

No matter how calmly I reassure her, Isabella howls with grief and incrimination, and I am only convinced that I must fly with Francesco to New York City to try my luck again. On the appointed morning, a drizzle of sleet flecks the surface of the Canalasso where I meet Francesco outside the hotel in San Marco where he has arranged for us to share a water taxi to the airport with four German tourists.

When I arrive, he is already on board, laughing with a female whose tight black curls fall from the furry edge of her hooded parka. Francesco reaches for my pack which he sets down beside the boatman, then nods for me to join him in the cabin. I leap onto the long leather seat beside him and smile somewhat awkwardly at the other passengers who speak excitedly as they click my picture.

Feeling the need to be alone with my beloved city, I excuse myself from the group and move to the open area in the back of the boat where I say goodbye to her bricks and crumbling mortar, goodbye to the moody waters of her canals, goodbye to a bed sheet stiff with the cold that hangs from a laundry line outside a lace covered window, goodbye to the old woman who smiles and waves as she waters a potted plant.

As we emerge from the mouth of the canal and cross the lagoon to Marco Polo Airport, the boat picks up speed and a crisp wind snaps back my ears. The young woman in the hooded parka joins me, saying something in her tongue to which I respond with a nod, pointing to the seat beside me.

With pleasure I watch her eyes light up with the jostling of the boat as laughter emerges from her lightly painted lips. And I think how one day I too will have a sleek boat and with Chiara beside me, I will speed across the lagoon, forcing laughter from deep within to conquer her sadness, welcoming all the possibilities of life and love that now await me on this new journey.

GLOSSARY

acqua alta: high water that occurs when the lagoon floods the low-lying areas of Venice for a few hours until the tide recedes, and locals mop up to resume their daily business.
bàcaro: small bar/eatery—specializing in the cicchetti prepared from fresh local ingredients, particularly seafood and vegetables bought that day in the market—washed down with an *ombra* of local wine.
bat mitzvah: the right of passage for Jewish females.
bella donna: beautiful woman
Tony Bennett: soulful Italian American singer born in Queens, New York, the son of immigrants from Calabria, Italy.
biscotti di regina: literally the queen's biscuits, named in honor of Margherita of Savoia, the second Queen of a united Italy, said to have possessed a sweet tooth.
Blue Note: legendary American record label that has preserved and promoted the work of jazz artists since 1939.
BQE: Brooklyn Queens Expressway, elevated stretch of roadway built in 1961, ideal for viewing water towers, fire escapes and flocks of pigeons swirling and diving over the rooftops of Brooklyn.
buku: slang for "a lot of" from French *merci beaucoup*, thank you very much; brought to the streets of New York by vets returning from the Vietnam War in the 1960s.
bupkis: slang for zero, nothing; from Yiddish *bubkes* meaning goat droppings.
Canalasso: Grand Canal, the ancient waterway that winds through Venice.
Canale di Cannaregio: one of 177 Venetian canals, connecting

over 115 islands, that runs through the district of Cannaregio.
Capiche: slang for you got that? from Italian *capisci?* meaning do you understand?
Ca'Rezzonico:17th century palazzo on the Grand Canal, today a museum dedicated to the works of Venetian masters, such as Gian Domenico Tiepolo, whose artworks include a portrait of Piccolo's ancestor.
John Coltrane: jazz saxophonist and composer whose music elevated human existence to a new height. "My music is the spiritual expression of what I am - my faith, my knowledge, my being."
Mark di Suvero: American poet of steel whose towering sculpture redefined public spaces around the world, ranging from a landfill in Queens to the canals of Venice.
Erberia: open-air fruit and vegetable market of Venice.
farcola: oar-post of the gondola, hand-carved preferably from walnut, cut and shaped to the measure of each oarsman.
ferro: ornamental metal blade at the oar of the gondola, cut with six bars, symbolic of the six districts of Venice.
Galleria dell'Accademia: originally an art school founded in 1750 on the Grand Canal, today this museum houses Venetian art from the 14th to 18th century.
Goodbye Pork Pie Hat: composition by Charles Mingus for Lester Young, recorded two months after his friend, legendary jazz musician Lester Young, died in 1959.
goombah: slang meaning longtime friend or associate.
Gowanus Canal: once a natural waterway, destroyed by over 200 years of industrial and human waste, the canal is the most polluted site in New York City, infamous for its oily surface and stench.
Hergé: penname of Belgium cartoonist, Georges Prosper Remi, creator of the 20th century series, *The Adventures of Tintin,* 23 graphic novels depicting the travels of an intrepid reporter with his equally intrepid dog, Snowy.
High Line: long and linear elevated park that runs along

Manhattan's westside, overlooking the Hudson River.
Luger's: short for Peter Luger Steakhouse, a venerable Brooklyn restaurant dating back to 1887.
ma che bella: what a beauty!
mannaggia: swear word that expresses frustration.
Andrea Mantegna: 15th century painter born in Padua renowned for his painting style that resembled classical sculpture.
la Marangona: oldest bell that rings out from the campanile of the Piazza di San Marco daily at noon and midnight.
Mercato di Rialto: the commercial hub of Venice located by the Rialto bridge, dating back to the 13th century.
Charles Mingus: virtuoso bass player, composer, band leader who when asked about his accomplishments said that his abilities as a bassist were the result of hard work but that his talent for composition came from God.
Mondo Nuovo: literally New World—the title of this 1791 painting by Gian Domenico Tiepolo—refers to the popular peep show of 18th century which through its manipulation of light and image, created exotic images that mesmerized its viewers—a descendant perhaps of cave paintings and a precursor of television and 21st century electronic devices.
paesano: literally villager, but also conveys the connection between people who feel that level of trust and camaraderie.
Pescaria: fish market on the Rialto for over 700 years.
la Piazza: constructed in the 9th home of the most iconic buildings of Venice, including the Basilica di San Marco, its bell tower, the ancient Palace of the Doge, as well as many pigeons.
Pulcinella: clowns from the Commedia d'el Arte tradition of the 17th century immortalized in the paintings of Giovanni Domenico Tiepolo.
Richard Serra: American sculptor whose gargantuan public works have generated controversy and international acclaim.
sestiere: district or division; six *sestieri* of Venice being

Cannaregio, San Polo, Dorsoduro, Santa Croce, San Marco, and Castello.

Giovanni Domenico Tiepolo: Venetian painter born in 1727 who worked under his acclaimed father Giovanni Battista Tiepolo while developing his own style of realism, natural simplicity and in later years, biting satire.

Tintoretto: 16th century Venetian master, Jacopo Robusti, praised and criticized by his contemporaries for the speed of his work and the bold brushstrokes of his style that earned him the title, *Il Furioso.*

Tintin in Tibet: published in 1958, 20th volume in the beloved series *The Adventures of Tintin* by Belgian cartoonist, Georges Prosper Remi, better known by his penname Hergé.

Vagilia: Christmas Eve

vaporetto: canal boats used for public transportation in Venice.

Villa Zianigo: Tiepolo's family villa for which he painted later works for their own viewing and pleasure, including the portrait of his studio assistant, Piccolo's ancestor on his mother's side.

WBGO: 88.3 FM, *Jazz 88*, public radio station located in Newark, New Jersey, broadcasting a life-giving stream of music for its adoring audience.

Lester Young: legendary tenor saxophonist, known for his unique blend of sophisticated harmonies and cool, free-floating style.

Acknowledgement

With deep thanks to Elias T. Ressler who as a pup created the character of an artistic Italian greyhound and his nemesis, Guy Gizzard. The sculpture depicted in this book as *Sniff* is an untitled steel work cut and welded by Ressler in a Williamsburg studio at the turn of this century.

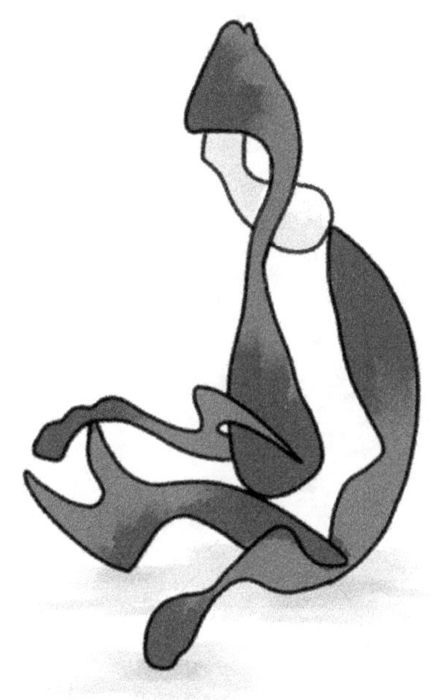

www.ingramcontent.com/pod-product-compliance
Lightning Source LLC
LaVergne TN
LVHW010913110826
845149LV00013B/2351
9798988586531